Search for the Golden Diamond of Kolimar

For La Von
my friend through
[illegible] and beyond!

Steve [illegible]

Also by Steve Dimeo

Nick Christmas Mysteries

The Magic Cape Caper

Search for the Golden Diamond of Kolimar

Search for the Golden Diamond of Kolimar

Nick Christmas Mysteries, Book 2

By

Steve Dimeo

HOLLISTON, MASSACHUSETTS

SEARCH FOR THE GOLDEN DIAMOND OF KOLIMAR

Cover Art by Rick Scheppel.

First printing September 2018
10 9 8 7 6 5 4 3 2 1

ISBN # 978-1-60975-221-7
ISBN (eBook) # 978-1-60975-222-4
LCCN # 2018946452

Silver Leaf Books, LLC
P.O. Box 6460
Holliston, MA 01746
+1-888-823-6450

Visit our web site at www.SilverLeafBooks.com

For lost jewels like you, Nettie,
that sparkle more in darkness.

Search for the Golden Diamond of Kolimar

When Diamonds are a Legend,
And Diadems—a Tale—
I Brooch and Earrings for Myself,
Do sow, and Raise for sale—

—#397, Emily Dickinson

1

Secure in knowing that the Magic Cape Caper might not be completely over—though we'd never know the fate of Dr. Bertram James and his wife Rae Anne for sure—we listened more carefully to the message left on the office answering machine.

A sultry female voice said, "I'm calling on behalf of Wade and Adeline Huntington to see if you could help locate the famous Golden Diamond of Kolimar which has gone missing from their estate. No news of this must leak to the media. The Huntington's have notified the insurance company but prefer getting the diamond back, since it's more than a keepsake, but one with great historical significance. Please return the call so I can set up an appointment to secure your services and discretion with a generous retainer."

"She didn't leave a phone number," said Randi, scratching down the caller ID information on one of her multi-colored post-it pads. "Hmm. She called from Evermore Title Company. Sounds kind of working class, doesn't it? Why is she calling for the owners?"

"That does seem odd." But I was mulling over the reference. "I wonder if it's *the* Kolimar Diamond."

"You've heard of it?"

"I know of only one from the lost Kolimar Mine of India that's 99 carats and thought to have been stolen from a revered statue that now bears some kind of curse."

"Oh, Nicky!" she said, hands clasped. "You're going to take this case, aren't you? Sounds like a great adventure!" She paused. "I wonder how she ever got your name."

I brushed knuckles at the lapel of my signature gray corduroy sports coat with its black leather elbows. "Our reputation?"

She grabbed a hand on the waist of her short pink skirt. "*What* reputation? We didn't exactly come out of the last case a rousing success."

I skewed my lips to the side. "Everything is always a work in progress."

"I guess 'losing' Dr. James kind of put us on the map, though."

"It did make headlines," I said. "You know what they say in Hollywood. Publicity is still publicity, even if it's bad."

We hadn't dared to share the real truth behind the caper, certainly not with the powers that be. We'd solved the mystery, but proved better at keeping a secret rather than divulging it. This was certainly the era of strange fame. What if we were now lumped together with the likes of O.J. Simpson, or worse, Paris Hilton and her crowd? I remembered with a frisson of horror one of Ms. Hilton's inadvertently astute observations about the absurdity of suicide bombers becoming the mode de jour when she posed the question, "Doesn't that *hurt*"?

"Why then," Randi asked with even keener perceptivity, "would she entrust us with locating such a famous diamond?"

"Good question," I agreed. Because we'd be more affordable having bungled the last case? But surely the Huntington's, owning such an expensive diamond, could afford anyone they wanted. She did promise a "generous retainer." Our nascent agency could sure use the cash.

"We need to see this potential client in person," said Randi, an eyebrow arched, "and find out what she really wants from us."

"You're learning, my dear. Make the appointment, but say we'll try to fit her in."

"I get it," she said coyly. "Play hard to get?"

"I presume you know how to do that."

She pursed her lips back at me. "I vaguely remember. But don't you have a promise to keep first?"

"I haven't forgotten," I said. "A nice dinner to celebrate the end of one case and the beginning of another?"

"I'll need time to get ready."

"You look fine right now."

She paused. "You don't know girls very well, do you."

"I vaguely remember," I rejoined with a smirk, remembering my late wife Angie, though she had learned to be prompt, while also training me to be more patient. "But that's also a work in progress."

"I can definitely lend a hand there."

"I imagine so."

"I'll see if she can make it tomorrow morning, then meet you back here at five?"

"You don't want me to pick you up at your place?"

"It's a mess like this desk," she said. "I need time to get everything back in order."

Then Randi dialed the number while I left the vestibule for the main office and stared in despair at the pile of papers knowing there had to be a desk somewhere underneath. That's where my detecting skills ended, though. I slapped hands at my side, giving up the daunting task of finding anything there yet. I turned and headed back to the oasis of Randi's reception area instead.

Randi had already hung up the phone but looked disappointed. "Well, that's interesting and a half."

I looked confused. "She couldn't make it?"

"She said it has to be after five tomorrow because she doesn't want anybody at her job to know she's hiring us." Then she studied my face and furrowed brow. "What's wrong, Nicky?"

"I'm intimidated, I guess, by the chaos on my desk."

"I'll tidy yours up soon, too, don't worry. I'm a good organizer when I set my mind to it."

"Randi to the rescue?"

"That's me!" she beamed at first before her lips curled in consternation.

"What's bothering you now?"

"Can you believe she calls herself 'Lady Vandemere,' insisting her husband's a 'Lord.' Isn't that a bit *presumptuous* here in America? And working for a title company yet? Where did wealthy people like Wade and Adeline Huntington *find* this girl anyway?"

I rubbed at my mustache. "Curiouser and curiouser."

"What are we in for here with her, Nicky?"

"Time enough to worry about that tomorrow when we meet this new 'lady.' For now, I need to introduce you to our own form of decadent pleasure, the nice dinner I promised."

"I can hardly wait!" said Randi, leaping up from her chair and hugging me. "Just you wait and see what I've got to show you this time! I'll make you proud you've got me here."

"Oh?" I said, thinking, Oh-oh, though.

Randi surprised me at least by showing up "only" two-and-a-half hours later a little after five. She wore a glittery silvery short party dress with a kick pleat front and back that made her look like a diamond herself, as I told her—except she admitted they were only rhinestones though I'd figured as much. "I think you're going to be a little—overdressed," I said sheepishly. Considering the amount of leg she exposed, I didn't think guys would mind.

She looked disappointed. "You said it's a nice place."

"Well, nic*er* than we've gone to before," I said trying to

wriggle out of this gracefully.

Then when we pulled up in front of Sunshine Pizza which I noticed from the sign was going out of business soon, Randi groaned. "Oh, Nicky, you *promised!*"

"If you're not happy here, sweetie," I said, "I'll make it up to you with something else. It's just that this is the only place in town that serves champagne with pizza—even if it's just Wycliff's. Isn't that classier than beer?" It had been a favorite place I'd frequented with my late wife Angie. But I added, "Give it a chance?"

She made a girlish "o" with her lips. "Okay, I guess."

The customers, young people though some looked to be in their thirties and forties, wore only scuffed Nikes, raggedy jeans made to look that way on purpose (an odd fad S. I. Hayakawa once labeled "synthetic poverty" though I guess if the tears were strategically placed could come across as subtly sexy) and baggy shorts with even baggier sweatshirts. "It's easy for people like us to shine that much more here." I said that in a half-question.

"I see what you mean now," she sighed, "that you're 'a work in progress.'"

"A diamond in the rough?"

"*Very* rough," she smiled, "but you can be buffed."

"Your specialty?"

"One of them," she smirked.

We started with the champagne while she examined the menu. I could see the wine even in plastic goblets settled both of us somewhat, her especially. "I guess the bubbly," she granted grudgingly later, "does make the margherita pizza go down better. They make the crust nice and crisp the way I like it. Too bad they're shutting down." When she drew the slice from her lips, a strand of cheese clung between the two I'd broken apart to give her, stringing it to my mouth, too. She looked down, dabbing a napkin at her lips self-consciously. A faint reminder of that classic scene from Walt Disney's "Lady and the Tramp" with the spaghetti noodle? That made me look down, too, embarrassed.

"A lot of good things go by the wayside," I allowed.

She looked at me, light blue eyes sparkling like the champagne working its magic. Ever the cockeyed optimist, she chanted back, "They can always be replaced with better ones."

2

Late the next day wearing a short pastel pink empire-cut spring dress with a sweetheart neckline and a white bolo jacket, Randi led our potential client into my "office" a quarter after five. She tried to hide a disgruntled glance at "Lady" Mena Vandemere's presumption again of an after-hours appointment. Mrs. Vandemere acted as if she weren't inconveniencing us the least bit, as she strode in on knee-high high-heeled black boots, sweeping long curly black hair away from speckled green eyes as if parting a veil while slinging part of her capelet from one shoulder. That revealed a swan-like neck and a scooped neckline adorned with gold chains dipping towards her endowments peeking out as crescents she seemed equally proud of. Talk about being over-dressed, not just for showing up at a detective agency, but having come like that from a Podunk job at a title insurance company?

When she took her seat in my old chair that sank down with her, the slit in her paisley dress parted, exposing smooth knees above the tops of her boots. She crossed her legs then, making gold bracelets clink like tambourines. "I'm the daughter representing my folks at their request," she explained right at the outset. "Where I'm working now is just a stopgap while I find something more suitable to my skills."

"Which would be?" I probed.

"I majored in arts and crafts, if you must know," she said haughtily, "but with a liberal arts degree I'm sure I'll find something much better when the market opens up more."

Well, at least she'd addressed the incongruity of someone with her "pedigree" settling for something relatively menial. "And your husband?" I said.

"Matthew is a loan officer at Oregon National Bank," she said. "But what does any of this have to do with the price of tea in China? Shouldn't you be asking about the crime?"

Well, that certainly wasn't very subtle. I forked fingers at my chin and leaned forward. "So how exactly did such a famous diamond 'go missing'?"

"My parents invited friends over to their manor last weekend for their fiftieth anniversary. They keep the diamond on display in what they call their Hall of Fame upstairs. It's been sealed in a locked acrylic case along with other valuables they've collected over the years from all over the world and now love to display as their travel trophies."

I hadn't asked for a preamble but got one anyway. She obviously meant to impress me that this would be no ordinary case we'd be taking on.

"Equipped with a security system?"

"Of course," she said. "But there was a thunderstorm that night and when the power went out after dinner, the back-up generator didn't engage right away. They have many objects d'art from exotic locales along with priceless paintings on the opposite side of the hall. The golden diamond, however, was the only thing stolen."

Electrical storms were rare here in the valley this time of year but not unknown. "Sounds like someone has a macabre sense of humor."

She pinched back one side of her wide Julia Roberts lips. "You mean what with the golden 'diamond' anniversary."

I nodded. Something still didn't seem right about this. "What went wrong with the generator?"

She lifted her sharp nose. "The wire connecting it to the main system had apparently frayed over time. That's since been repaired. But the power came back on anyway after three hours or so. We didn't discover the diamond gone until the next morning."

I leaned forward. "And the cleaning staff?"

"All trusted employees above reproach," she sniffed again. "The Huntingtons are very generous with their help. The cook has been with them the twenty years they've been retired."

I flipped my notepad closed with a flair of finality. "You wouldn't object if we check them out ourselves?"

"Of course not," she said, "though I think it's the wrong avenue."

That was an easy lead-in to my daily fee of $500 plus expenses, against an initial deposit of a grand that would ensure our services.

I thought I saw her arch a very thin eyebrow at that spiel, assuring her I would keep her informed of the running tally as long as it took us to find the item. She wrote out the check, balancing the leather book on her knee despite it being awkwardly raised as low as she sank in the cushion. She pushed herself up off the chair, adjusting her skirt hem which had slid up some because of my careworn chair and offered me the payment. I glanced at it enough to see that it wasn't her personal account but rather her parents', but with her signature—and that she'd made it out for $10,000. "You'll start first thing tomorrow?"

"Yes indeedy," I agreed maybe a little too heartily, buoyed by the bonus.

"I should warn you," she added, "that the insurance adjuster from Starmark Fidelity will be prowling around, too, preparing her report on the theft should you not be able to find it in a timely fashion."

I raised my own eyebrows at the mention of "her." It was still unusual to find a female adjuster specializing in diamonds even these days. "How much was it insured for?"

"Twenty million," she said, "though it could be worth more because of its peculiar color and quality despite the controversy over the 'enhancement' of its hue."

I gulped. I had a fleeting fear we might be out of our league here but didn't want to come off as the rube from Ashborough—though that's how I felt. Still, that large of a deposit imbued me with renewed courage to prove our mettle in spite of our agency's infancy. "I'd have to confer with the adjuster anyway in the course of this investigation."

"Of course," she said warily.

A lot of "of courses" there, hoping our own course towards the resolution wouldn't be as circuitous. I presented her with my card about the way she'd proffered the check to me—dubiously.

"Please bring more official ID to the gate of the manor when you arrive," she said. "I won't be available during the weekday to introduce you formally."

"S-O-P," I assured her. When she tilted her head at me, I translated. "Standard operating procedure for licensed detectives."

Lady Mena Vandemere then raised her eyebrows again at my tone, twisting her lips as if she'd bitten into something sour. It took a while, I guess, for clients to warm up to my brand of acerbic wit which cropped up at the most unexpected moments. While a detective all those years at the county Sheriff's Department, I'd always tried to subscribe to the Jack Webb school of detection from my father's days of the "Dragnet" era—"Just the facts, ma'am"—but often with a seasoning of cynical skepticism.

I couldn't help wondering, for instance, whether she was merely standing up for her parents, or whether personal interests lay behind her apparent altruism. Call me suspicious, but...well, just call me suspicious. As I'd already tried to impress on Randi, it came with the territory. Trusting too much in this business could prove hazardous to one's health.

Learned pupil that she was, Randi expressed the same sentiment after Lady Vandemere sashayed out of our Spartan furnishings by saying simply, “Kinda uppity, isn’t she?”

We both peered down through the window as she headed towards her car parked on the curb, an older red Mustang that looked like an original Shelby. A pretty expensive cachet for one working merely for a title company. Or could this be more her husband’s choice?

Then she turned around to see us both standing there in the window like a poor imitation of Grant Wood’s “American Gothic” portrait. She shouted something that we had to wind open the side casement window to hear her repeat. “You wouldn’t be able to wrap up this investigation by Father’s Day, by any chance, would you?” That was June 21st less than a week away.

“What’s the rush?” I said, over an unrealistic expectation.

“My folks want to follow up their anniversary with a ceremony at the church renewing their vows that Sunday. It’d be a nice gift for them.”

And a feather in our cap if we could make it. “That’ll push it, lady.” I tried not to make the title come across as caustic.

“There’ll be a bonus of five grand if you can,” she said with a wave swiveling her hand that reminded me of the way a beauty queen might do before a crowd from a parade convertible.

“We’ll do our best,” I promised with a toothy smile that I hoped looked sincere accompanied by a folksy wave of both hands, fingers gangling widely. That was more to offset hers.

Randi stared at me with a cluck. "You definitely need help in the PR department."

"I thought I handled myself as a consummate professional."

"About as convincing as a card shark," she laughed, "except you weren't wearing the shark-skin suit."

"Nice to have a cheerleader."

"Always ready to come to the aid of your party," she said. "But I'd sure operate better on a full stomach."

I pretended to be taken aback though, yes, I'd heard her stomach rumbling cutely again. "I don't want you to get the wrong idea, Randi, that I'm your Sugar Daddy."

"Your lavish dinner of pizza last night," she said, "made me think otherwise, partner."

Oh, my. She certainly gave as good as I dished out. "Don't forget the champagne," I said in my defense as we both left the office with her locking up. "Hey, wait a minute." I perked up as I remembered that handle she'd added as a fillip. "'Partner'?"

"Remember," she said pulling back the sleeve of her blouse, as if getting ready to work rather than preparing to leave, "I've already proved myself more than just a receptionist."

"'Gal Friday' doesn't cover all the bases?"

"Enough," she said as she gave me that toodle-oo girlie wave of her fingers on her way to her yellow Chevy Malibu, "is never enough!"

"What have I gotten myself into?" I said in mock despair. She pointed to where Lady Vandemere had parked in front of the unassuming brick two-story building which was still mostly vacant. "Exactly what I was thinking about this case."

"I can see I'm going to have to pony up another offering."

She tilted her head. "It better not be McDonald's or a pizza parlor."

I had to scramble for ideas here since I wasn't used to a "partner" like this. "How about fish and chips at a local watering hole?"

"What kind of 'hole'?"

"That's exactly what it's called, The Watering Hole." Ashborough's eating establishments never boasted particularly imaginative monikers. I nodded at the place across the street. "It's along the same lines as The Grinder. Still, the food's pretty good."

She hesitated, visibly weakened by the mention of fish and chips, a hand grabbed at her waist. "A peace offering?"

I smirked. "Call it what you want."

She seemed to be mulling over the possibilities. "Is the fish cod or halibut?"

"Your choice. Both are on the menu."

"A good sign," she wavered.

"And like The Grinder, they do make their own desserts."

"Hot apple pie?"

"'Hot'?"

"That's the way I like it—preferably with a slice of American cheese."

I preferred it cold—and served a la mode. "So—you're

tempted?"

"Maybe," she said, her lips in a Brigitte Bardot moue, eyes downcast. I think she meant to act reluctant—though it struck me more as coquettish. "We should start off this caper on the right foot. For one thing, you need someone to watch over you when it comes to a 'lady' like this one."

Sometimes she could look so child-like even while posing as my would-be paladin though I considered it more my job to watch over her. Still, I found it charming. Not that I'd dare tell her that. "Added to your job description?"

"You need to realize," she said almost playfully, "just what women are capable of."

"I'm getting a pretty good notion already," I laughed at her knowing smirk.

During our dinner, I elaborated. "You think we're up to a case of this magnitude?"

"Don't underestimate us, Mr. Christmas," she countered. "Remember, I wasn't born yesterday."

"Almost!" I joked back. We'd both had a glass of wine with our fish and chips that had again loosened our tongues.

She actually giggled. "Just because I'm young doesn't mean I don't have a few tricks up my sleeve—and other things."

"We can't have too many surprises," I chastened.

"Believe me, Nicky, you're going to like the ones I come up with this time around! But I think Lady Mena has something more up her very stiff back, too, besides that stick!"

"Very well put!" I laughed. "But together, my dear, we're about to find out."

3

Randi bounced in early again the next morning, her short pastel pink summer dress flouncing as she spun into the office, whisking the door closed so that the dimpled frosted glass panel rattled. Dad told me that's what Loretta Young used to do in the opening segment of her TV show back in the Fifties when he was just a kid. I'd seen snippets of it on YouTube.

"I'm ready to go at it again," she said, a little too gaily for me, this despite my getting there in time to make my Starbucks French Roast, which I offered her, blinking at her excessive early morning ebullience with a combination of wonder and befuddlement. Had I ever been this joyous myself? Maybe at first with Angie's encouragement. Now, though, youth seemed more like a dreamy mirage. But hers was more an induction coil whose energy field touched me even more than the coffee. Still, coffee was a known fall-back. I'd wait to see if the other kicked in.

"And take a look at this!" She lifted up the hem of her skirt on her right side to reveal a black lace garter at her thigh and, lo and behold, a matching holster with the Kel-Tek P-11 pistol strapped inside. All I *really* saw, though, was her naked thigh.

My jaw dropped. This definitely did have a kick to it! She indeed had other tricks up her sleeve all right—though what was under that dress seemed far more entrancing. I'd certainly caught the electric current streaming from her—and then some. In one of my less voluble states, I managed to stutter out only, "Uhhh—"

"Oh, you guys!" she said. "The gun shop owner did the same thing when I tried it on just to make sure it wouldn't slip. You're all so *easy!*" She brushed the skirt portion back down. "This one doesn't need a strap clipped to my panties like older versions but wraps about my thigh with just a Velcro clasp. Sometimes, though, it loosens or catches on my dress or the lining. It would on a slip, too, if I still wore them, but that static cling made them always ride up on me."

"Wouldn't it be better," I finally said, knowing too well how strange it was to be having a conversation like this with a "partner" like no other, "to have one you could tighten with a belt like a shoulder holster?"

"Normally I can snug this one up just fine," she answered with a pat at the inside of her thigh. "Sometimes even leather or fabric belts loosen, if you get too cold. I just have to be careful this one doesn't ride down when I'm running." She then lifted the hem again a tad. "Besides, the lace matches the rest of my underwear." She paused demurely—or coyly. It was hard to tell. "You'll have to take my word for it."

"I believe you," I croaked.

She fluffed the skirt back down, taking out the rumpling from her fabulous sneak preview.

"My God, Randi," I finally gasped, realizing I was having trouble catching my breath. "We're only going to interview the old couple and their help. They've just celebrated their fiftieth. It's not like we're meeting the Mafia's capo de capo!"

"Well, I'm ready anyway if they've got some dastardly villain lurking in the closet somewhere that they don't know about," she said with typical melodramatic zeal. "I decided to go all-out on this because midway through that last case you let me join you on those interviews. This way I can be more chic—or is it chic-er? I don't want to look like a gangster's moll or some old-time PI's floozy."

Actually, though, as I gazed at her with that swirly dress and its frilly lace trim on the short arms and hem, she did look like a more updated femme fatale that could have stepped off the garish cover of a Mickey Spillane novel. And her using the word "floozy"? Was this girl for real or a renegade from some film noir—though far more colorful and "springier"? I looked down at my sports coat and wondered if I should try to locate my old double-breasted version of this coat so I could fit in with *her*. What was she doing, damaging my image—or enhancing it? I was beginning to think more the latter now—and that, too, was scary.

"Why don't you let me update your old boring message on the phone, and make it a little livelier?"

I think my mouth was still open before I could respond when she started to do that by sitting in her armed receptionist's chair with one leg informally tucked under her (I could see her—and even her gun the way the dress puckered up—through the hole in the cheap desk much like my own) and worked the keys to change the recording.

"Christmas Detective Agency—where it's Christmas every day!" she frothed. "There! How's that?"

"You make it sound like a Hallmark card."

"Well, what's wrong with that? You need more pizzazz to perk up this place—like all these drab furnishings, especially these dreary drapes over the blinds—so it doesn't look so funky. You've got it like the inside of a gypsy's booth or a dusty bookstore than a classy detective's home base. And I'm just the gal to spruce things up for you."

Wasn't she too young to use the term "spruce up," too? Still, her elation was infectious. She must have felt there was still hope for me yet. She added, "Maybe after I deposit this check we can think about getting started on a little refurbishing?" The days of catalogues were long past, sadly, but there was Amazon and the internet—and still good old-fashioned shopping store to store, every man's nightmare. "I can help you there, as well, with some old-fashioned shopping." Was she reading my mind? "I have a flair for decorating," she prattled on. "I've dabbled a bit in that, you know. With a B.A. in business, I figured I could do almost anything—and interior designing always fascinated me. Didn't you even look at my resume?"

Again she'd cut me to the quick. I couldn't tell her I'd given it only a perfunctory once-over once she'd come in looking like a million bucks in that blue business suit with its V-neck jacket over a short pencil skirt and matching high-heeled shoes that she'd kind of wobbled on. She'd put her finger on it when she'd said we're guys—and easy. "Maybe after we get more of a handle on this case, I'll—" How to put this? "—let you loose?"

"Oh, could we, Nicky? It'll be a dream shopping with me, you'll see." A dream? Where had she come from anyway, some time warp? She'd said it, though, so naturally as if she'd already won the lottery. Maybe she had—or, was it possible, *I* had? Note how cleverly she'd inveigled me into the equation?

For now, though, after we stopped at my credit union and had her sign a card to show she was my "confidential secretary" and could make transactions on the account on her own in the future, I drove us to the West Hills to visit the Huntingtons in person. The gated house sloped down northward off Cornell Road overlooking a narrow tributary of Rock Creek threading along the back of a long two-acre lot. (We'd Googled it first, naturally, fold-out maps that could never be refolded again a welcome thing of the past.)

"Mena told us you'd be by first thing this morning," said the deep voice over the speaker at the brick post before the rounded iron gate with an ornate "H" at its center opened. When it swung open, I was reminded oddly of a flapper in one of those old pinball machines from my youth before video games replaced them. I only hoped we'd be the player, not the pinball—though after Randi's sneak peek I already had my doubts. "And here you are already. Nine on the dot."

So he had answered it himself, not a butler. I just looked over at Randi who jounced up and down in her seat, hands knitted together excitedly. "A real-live mansion!" she effused.

"Or 'manor,'" I reminded her to honor the chosen argot Lady Vandemere had so superciliously used.

We pulled up in my "peasant" of a Toyota Sienna XLE under the *porte cochere* that reached out to the lavish Italian three-tiered fountain splashing beside us before I rounded the van to let Randi out like a gentleman. First impressions mattered—and so did manners.

Wade Huntington stood at the raised panel French doors marked by an oval stained-glass window depicting the sun. He was wearing a sporty navy-blue cardigan over a golf shirt, white chinos and white canvas loafers. He was adjusting the brim of his tweed newsboy cap before removing it and clutching it in his left hand to reveal a head of fluffy white hair when I held Randi's hand to help her out and brought her up to greet him.

"Wow," she said out the side of her mouth on the way. "Gentlemen everywhere! I could get used to this."

"Appreciate it while it lasts," I whispered as I led her up the stairs.

I displayed my PI license to make it all official though he waved it off without examining the card. "I know you were a county detective before you went independent."

Then he stepped aside to introduce his wife Adeline who greeted us with more of a strained smile. She looked tired but wore her own white hair pulled to the side in a French braid that fell down her summery ecru caftan. "Welcome, welcome," she said, backing away to let her husband guide us to the vaulted family room off the gourmet kitchen where an Hispanic lady wearing a yellow bandana was busying herself at the commercial-grade gas stove. They introduced us to Maria Valesquez who nodded politely but couldn't approach us since she was peeling and cutting up onions into a large frying pan.

The soaring clerestory glass windows that spanned the family room and part of the kitchen beyond the maple cabinets opened out to a vast deck overlooking a sweeping swale that ended in the silvery glimmering of the creek at the site's northernmost boundary. An Oriental gardener putted along on a riding lawn mower back and forth beyond an infinity pool that glittered with no apparent edge (whence its name) dripping over into the channel that re-fed the water back into the pool. It looked so placid and untouched as if it had never been used. The wood-framed screen door—a Pella, I noted—was open though it wasn't quite that warm yet this early in the morning.

"Oh, it's just lovely!" Randi said.

"Thank you, dear," said Adeline who insisted we call her "Addy." "Would you like tea or coffee?"

She asked it more of Randi than of me as if the women were already about to withdraw to the "drawing" room while the men went about "men" things. That at least fit into an antiquated propriety as I'd expected from seasoned wealth like this. Randi seemed to take it all in with wide-eyed wonder. "Coffee would be great," she said with a glance over at me, blinking her crystal blue eyes that told me she'd prefer to stay by my side but acknowledged she'd follow Addy's lead.

"Would you like to see our Hall of Fame right off the bat?" he said directly to me, pointing up.

"We'll join you in a bit," Addy assured us as we climbed the curved stairway to a mezzanine where a reading alcove marked the landing. We turned right into the hallway that featured their collections lining one side, the other side displaying startling original oil paintings as Mena Vandemere had mentioned.

He noticed my attention as I squinted to read the brass plates under the two paintings. I'd been afraid I'd be needing more than just reading glasses soon. Sadly, this confirmed it. He was nice enough to pick up the gauntlet for my sake. "I'm not just the ex-hippie hometown baker everybody thinks I am. I actually put in the winning bid at Christie's for this famous Jean-Léon Gérôme painting of Galatea, still partly a statue, bending over to give her creator Pygmalion a passionate kiss. It's one of three he did of the same thing—not counting his own sculpture that William Randolph Hearst purchased for his castle. Compare that with this modern one by Boris Vallejo of the sculptor only kissing the hand of the nude still in the process of changing from stone to flesh and blood. One an invaluable masterpiece, the other an American painting I bought at a smaller gallery that I think will only appreciate with time. You must come to the next showing at the Pearl Gallery in a couple of weeks. Our own community offers gems of its own right under our noses, if people would just give local artists a chance."

I'd stopped in at one gallery on the way to Lincoln City with Angie though it featured only competent but fairly mundane seascapes. "I'd like to. Randi would, that's for sure."

He looked at me with an avuncular smile, maybe seeing more in that addition that I didn't think I meant. "I'll wrangle you two an invitation then, regardless of this investigation's outcome."

"Why are you so interested, Wade, in this myth over others?"

"Aren't we all creators in a way falling in love with what we make—whether it's children, bread—or vibrant artifacts like this?" He indicated now the beauty on display in the transparent cases to the right and the various jewel-encrusted scabbards and daggers hanging above them, a shiny longbow and classic, brilliantly polished rifles and muskets, each with easier-to-read brass plates noting their estimated dates and provenance. A couple of golden ceremonial masks that looked Siamese or Indonesian also flanked the weapons. I realized as I followed him, he smelled faintly of British Sterling, Dad's favorite after shave. "Offended in my own time," Dad used to quip from the "legend in your own time" slogan.

"These stand more," he went on, "as glorified symbols of power that changed the world, not always for the better." He pointed with a gnarled finger at the weapons in particular. "This vintage longbow helped the English win the Hundred Year's War against France in the 14th century while the Colt model 1855 revolving rifle here, despite its tendency to chain-fire, almost single-handedly helped the Union army defeat the Confederates." We stopped finally at the case before the closed doors beyond, the hallway's end marked by a white built-in breakfront. The black velvet was rumpled inside now empty but for the label which read "The Kolimar Diamond." "Even famous gems like this one meant to make the reigning royalty at the time stand above the rest. Although it's said to have once been larger and part of a towering statue of a goddess in the distant past, it's thought to have adorned the turban of Maharaja Ranjit Singh when he took over India under the aegis of the British Empire at the start of the 19th century, too." Then he looked up at me. "But of course it's beautiful in its own right, a rare stone we've etched into an even rarer beauty with a golden tint that makes it even more spectacular. Experts say it had a strange red flaw at its center that, frankly, you could only make out if you turned it just right. Addy saw it more easily than I could." A pause as he lowered his head. "We miss it terribly."

"What's behind this wall?" I said.

"Mena's old bedroom kept the way she left it. Ours is just next door. Neither of us hears the way we used to but we're pretty sure whoever took it didn't make much noise removing it during the night. The house is well soundproofed, though, with plenty of batting in the walls we made thicker than usual. We oversaw the construction but the architect honored our priorities to a fault."

I examined the lock on the case which looked pristine. It

hadn't obviously been jimmied open—or if it had, it had been slickly accomplished. Next to it still lay a golden mask that looked Egyptian. I pointed to it. "Why didn't they take the other valuables like this one?"

"Good question," he said.

I was also a little surprised the thief or thieves hadn't replaced it with an imitation. "And no request for a ransom?"

"Not a word," he said. "It's just—gone."

We heard the women moil up the stairs, Randi helping Addy by holding onto her arm, then head towards us. Randi took her time ogling the collection in the case more than the weapons and masks festooning the wall overhead, the nudes on the wall to the left warranting a glance that made her blush. The Gérôme painting was especially erotic with that loving kiss.

"You've got some beautiful memories here," Randi finally said pointing to the cases, wide-eyed at the shimmering stones.

"It's too bad our travels came to an end," Addy responded wistfully. She slipped up beside Wade who wrapped his strong bare arm around her while she hunched easily against his chest almost lost there because of her small size.

Randi backed away more towards me as she stared at the wife. "They don't have to be, do they?"

She looked paler in her husband's thin shadow. "We're getting too old to put up with the travails of trying to fight with the airlines these days just to make even short trips, let alone ones halfway around the world. It's not the same since 9/11."

I noticed the counter midway down from the cabinet at the end of the hall featured a photo of the two of them, presumably their wedding photo with a sepia tint, both dressed in what seemed street clothes rather than typical wedding attire. "No family photos?"

"We only had Mena," said Wade. "It's short for 'Philomena.' Calling her 'Phil' like we did Addy's mother didn't seem right for her."

"I couldn't have any more after her," Addy explained.

I paused. "We'd like to interview your servants, too."

Wade gave a half nod. "I don't think they'll help much. They're as baffled as we are at the robbery—and almost as heart-broken, I think. It was a beautiful fixture here for years." He made it sound like a person.

Addy broke away from him, hands knotted as she adjusted her wristwatch and tapped its face as a reminder to her husband. He arched a bushy white eyebrow and turned towards us. "I hope you don't get in each other's way but the insurance adjuster plans to drop by later this morning. Called first thing this morning, assuring us she was GIA certified and eminently qualified. She sounds young. I think that's why she reeled off her credentials."

"Nice to know," I shrugged, "that even the Gemological Institute of America attracts women now."

Addy pulled out a slip of paper from one of the large patch pockets in her caftan. "Said her name was Sari Maravar. Sounds Indian, doesn't it. I guess she would know even better than most the worth of a diamond from her ancestral country."

"We'll let her do her job while we do ours," I tried to assure them though I saw potential problems looming. I hoped to get the interrogation of the staff out of the way today before "interviewee fatigue" set in. That often led to too many overlooked details that could prove crucial to the investigation. "All the more reason to get started now."

Randi piped up with, "How about with the cook? She's still right there in the kitchen."

I looked at her, wondering if it was because of the proximity to the cooking rather than an investigator's instinctive curiosity. "In the meantime," I said, "could we maybe get a list from your butler of the guests you had for dinner that night?"

"We don't really have a butler per se," said Wade. "But Peter Travers, our chauffeur, fills in as one on the rare occasions we need him to. That night he offered. But so few showed out of the many we invited, he didn't stay around long. You might be more interested in the guest list, especially those we never even heard back from."

"How many showed?" Randi had to ask.

"Just my daughter and her husband and the neighbors next door," said Wade, the disappointment evident in the lines on his face.

I followed with, "Out of how many?"

"Twenty. Isn't that something? I'd always wondered what if we threw a party and nobody came? Now, thanks to the questionable joys of old age, I do."

But, I thought, the *thieves* had somehow skulked in—and boldly while the hosts and their guests bumbled about in the storm's darkness downstairs.

4

Sharing a stunned look at each other, Randi and I descended the stairs, the couple following behind more slowly. Wade strolled out to the deck and headed for the garage. Addy started working *The Oregonian*'s daily crossword puzzle on the dining room table. That distracted Randi momentarily who'd interested our last client in the hobby. "Oh, you like doing them, too?"

Addy half-grinned, tapping the pencil at her temple. "Keeps the mind sharp. At my age, I need all the help I can get."

"I just do it," said Randi, "because it makes me feel like I'm getting something accomplished while I'm waiting around for something else to happen."

"You won't have to worry about that today," I smiled.

"I know!" she said. "Is it okay if I start first on Maria?"

I shrugged. Who was I to stand in the way of a zealous

novice? "Knock yourself out," I grinned.

"Besides," she leaned into me with a hand beside her mouth, "maybe I can learn Maria's secret to a good pot roast while I'm at it."

I had to precede her by showing my license to make it official, but she followed through with surprising zest as I took a back seat, simply nodding as she proceeded. But Maria didn't offer much because her quarters stood at the easternmost end of the house with a separate entrance "like casita," she explained. That put her too far away to have heard anything significant since the theft took place after she'd served the dinner and cleaned up the kitchen just before the power went out when that forced her to retire early and the guests to leave. "I hear cars go is all," she concluded, "Miss Mena stay because she show Mr. Wade and Miss Addy to bedroom with flashlight."

"Then when did they discover the diamond was missing?" Randi asked.

"Not till next morning when Addy cry out."

Afterwards on our way to the garage to interview Peter Travers, I said, "So they walked right past the display case—and didn't notice anything wrong?"

"It was dark, Nicky," she said. "Why would they have thought to check when they were just trying to make their way to their bedroom?"

"So we don't know for sure when it actually disappeared," I said.

Peter Travers couldn't shed much light either on the details of the evening during the storm. We caught him while he was out polishing the silver Mercedes Benz Sprinter in his cut-offs and worn Nikes and not much else, which Randi took in a little too conscientiously. He came around the front of the luxury hybrid SUV and gave us both a hearty handshake, the hand sporting a large gold ring with what looked like an onyx, making his solid pecs barely jitter with the motion. “Glad to meet a real live PI and his good-looking sidekick,” he said with a deep baritone that made him sound like Howard Keel except for the tinge of Irish brogue. His eyes twinkled their deep blue which Randi noted, too, me not taking too kindly to her attention and his eyeing her back with his smoky look. The large carriage house with its garage doors rolled open revealed a bisque-colored Cadillac Escalade inside, the Huntingtons’ show of wealth evident more in their choice of vehicles than in their folksy demeanor. “I just had to make sure everyone got through the gate since I had to open it manually without the power on. I’m the one that checked the generator and jerry-rigged the frayed wire so it came back on a little before the regular power did. I was pretty tired when I went to bed upstairs in my attic studio. We didn’t hear about the theft until the next day.”

“You heard nothing out of the ordinary going on outside during all this time?” I said.

“Well, maybe that deer back again, though I didn’t check to make sure. The animals come down off the mountains after a lean winter like we had. I’ve had to run off the doe and her two fawns more than once from the small garden beyond the pool. It’s too far away to set off the backyard alarm."

I had Randi give him one of our cards. "We may be changing the face of the cards soon, right Nicky?"

"Some faces don't need changing," he grinned broadly at her, making her blush which is what he was trying to do, staying shirtless to boot, the cad.

I cleared my throat. "Thanks, Mr. Travers. It's going to seem like déjà vu for you when the insurance adjuster comes by later. She may ask the same questions."

"She?" he said, thick eyebrows as his ridged brow was wriggling. They were almost as brown as his very tanned chest with its T-shaped splotch of curly hair.

"Expertise cuts across the sexes these days," I said as I waved the list of invitees he'd given me in air and thanked him. The list included addresses and phone numbers but no emails. The invitations must have been sent out more formally by snail mail.

"Vincent and Katalena Hadid from next door were the only people that showed, you know, besides Mena and her husband. I felt bad for the Mr. and Mrs. But Mr. Wade—he tends to take things more in stride lately. Me? I would have been pretty upset myself."

"Any idea why so few came?" said Randi.

He eyed her up and down. "Maybe that predicted storm in some cases—though I have my own suspicions. The Huntingtons don't like to socialize as much as they used to, for one. But I think it's 'Lady Mena' the guests were staying away from. There's been some friction in the family since her marriage. But the Mr. and Mrs. are really well-liked where they volunteer."

I asked for examples.

"Food bank for him, the women's auxiliary at the hospital for her. And they attend things like the Doernbecker Hospital ball every year. They manage to keep themselves busy, I have to hand it to them there."

Randi probed for more possibilities. "He doesn't associate much with the people from his company?"

"Not since he sold the bread business to that conglomerate," he said. "The Huntingtons prided themselves on their whole-grain breads before it became the fad it is today, but I guess it was hard work and long hours for too many years. I didn't come on the scene until five years ago, long after they made that sale and retired full-time to this house that they built some twenty years ago or so, when Mena was still living here. But I love taking care of such great cars for whenever they need them. Sometimes I take Maria to market when she has to restock the pantry. I'm pretty lucky to land a job like this for such good people."

"You do seem to be in your element," I said. "Well, give us a call if you think of anything else that comes to mind later."

"Will do, Mr. Christmas," he said with a salute that was more military than friendly. Randi watched him out the corner of her eyes, I think suspecting he'd do the same to her again, but instead he focused more on polishing the car. Unrequited love, I quietly sighed, not for the car that kept him so dutifully preoccupied but grateful to him for spurning Randi at the end.

That left us one more staff member to interview—Lon Sung. He was in back at the machine shed then cleaning the riding mower's blades and dumping the leavings into the recycle bin there when we came up to him, unintentionally startling him. He took off his orange John Deere cap and wiped his forehead with the sleeve of the green jump suit he wore to protect his street clothes. We could see the white shirt he wore beneath because the suit's zipper was pulled down, it already growing warm this early.

"I don't stay here at night like Pete and Maria," he said sounding very much an educated American, not an immigrant, "but I did put up the canopy to protect the guests from the sun or the rain, this time both—though I wasn't around for the thunderstorm. It proved a lot of bother for the few who showed, but I did what they asked me to. They're easy to work for, so I often do more than they ask."

Despite his name, he said he was born in Portland and grew up here, although his parents he admitted somewhat shame-faced, still spoke only broken English. I could relate only in that my Italian grandparents had done the same, not my second-generation folks. A wiry man, he wore gloves that looked oversized almost like boxing gloves before he removed the right one to shake hands with us, making a full bow from his waist towards Randi. He addressed us more formally by our last names, too, seeming more comfortable with that as Peter had.

"What time did you leave the premises then?" I said.

"After their daughter arrived. I could see the thunderheads rising up in the east and made sure the poles were securely fastened to the stakes. Once I knew they didn't need me for anything else, I left for home, cautioning them not to let the flaps down if the wind whipped up too much or they might make the tent unstable."

"And when did you return?" Randi said.

"First thing next morning before eight to take down the canvas. That's when I learned about the stone disappearing." He had a habit of clamping his lips to a thin line after answering, looking as if he were holding back from saying too much. It could have been because he was trying to be overly polite, though, or his nervousness at having his loyalty questioned at all. Or maybe his heritage. Sometimes that was more inherent than people acknowledged. He took off his cap again and scratched his raven black hair which flopped straight over his short forehead when he did. "Strange thing, that."

Randi pricked up her ears, tilting her head. "What's so strange about it?"

"Why now?" he said. "They've had these people over before so I doubt it's any of them. But if it's a stranger, he must have been casing the place quite a while before this. And pulling it off during a storm which just happens to cause a power outage when the generator doesn't automatically switch on? A lot of coincidences."

"You think it's someone who lives near here then?" I said.

He positioned the cap more firmly onto his head with both hands before putting back on his gloves. "Wouldn't you?"

"They had neighbors in attendance at the party," said Randi, musing.

"They're 'regulars,' though," said Lon.

I picked up on that. "'Regulars'?"

"Card partners," Lon answered. "They play pinochle the first Monday of each month—though Mrs. Huntington complains that the Hadids cheat mercilessly. Mr. Huntington thinks it's funny how obviously they signal each other—you know, sometimes pounding at their hearts to indicate their strongest suit or making a shoveling gesture to imply spades, that kind of thing. I'd find it irritating myself but he's always looking for the good in people—and getting a kick out of what others would consider irritating. Unusually forgiving, if you ask me."

"How long's this been going on" I said, "this 'friendship'?"

"Fairly recent," said Lon as he finished filling the yard debris receptacle and wheeled it under the eaves, us following. "Late last fall maybe? They brought over one of those good neighbor fruit baskets like the Welcome Wagon. Very old school—but that's the Huntingtons for you." He got into his faded green Toyota truck. "Anything else?"

"Not right now," I said.

"I've got to pick up some more yard supplies to treat the lawn and keep the dandelions down, but I'll be back if you need me later."

I thanked him as he backed away from the shed and headed for the circular driveway sloping up to the gate.

"I presume the Hadids are next?" said Randi, eyes gleaming since she thought these neighbors had suddenly become prime suspects. I wondered about motivation, though, since they lived in a large stucco house with two turrets in a Moroccan motif next door that looked as much an estate as the Huntingtons'.

Still, they sounded like strange companions for the likes of the Huntingtons, especially if they played so fast and loose at cards. The Huntingtons, for all their down-to-earth ways, still seemed too strait-laced to put up with such shenanigans—unless they were desperate for jesters to entertain them. A lot to risk for a laugh or two with such a valuable collection on display.

I hadn't exactly excluded Mr. Sing either. The way he talked had seemed too—well—elocutionary, frankly, for his station. Even the well-educated sometimes preferred working with their hands more, so his dedication wasn't entirely unexpected. He did seem to respect the Huntingtons', maybe because they'd come from the ranks of blue collar workers themselves, accruing their wealth honestly through hard work and parsimony in the time-honored American tradition. I couldn't blame him for his admiration. The Huntingtons were hard not to like—which made this theft seem all the more egregious.

5

As we got back in the van and started to buckle up, another car pulled up behind us, a white sporty Ford Escort.

"The insurance adjuster?" said Randi.

"We'd better introduce ourselves first," I sighed, "and get that out of the way. We want her to be a help, not a hindrance."

Randi pursed her lips cutely again. "That's probably what she's thinking about us—if she knows the Huntingtons have us working already to get the jewel back."

I smirked. "I guess that means we have to put our best gumshoe forward."

She raised a foot to show off her white Romanesque sandals vining up her shapely calves from wedged heels. "Speak for yourself."

We got back out and sauntered over towards her as she stepped out, tall and svelte in a work uniform that didn't do justice to her figure, and reached into the back for her valise.

We went up to her as the hatch hummed shut. The side of the car bore an insignia of a stylized star with the name "Starmark" curved over its top and "Fidelity," its script snaking beneath. She stood upright, her long straight black hair trailing past her slender shoulders over a khaki work shirt with a sharp collar and matching pants that bagged at the top and tapered towards work boots that looked too big for her, laces loose on one of her feet.

"You wouldn't be Sari Maravar, would you?" I said with a courteous bow.

"I would," she said, her dark almond eyes with naturally long lashes looking at me and Randi askance, not sure whether we were friend or foe. An adjuster must feel about as welcome as someone in our field, her judgments probably not making either the insured or her company entirely happy. "And you would be?"

So I did the intros, realizing the Huntingtons had *not* warned her of our appearance here. Of course they hadn't yet met us. I made sure Ms. Maravar knew we didn't need to stand on ceremony, that she could call us by our first names.

"Yes, by all means," she said suspiciously. "You can call me Sari, too."

"So what do you tell your clients when you come up with your estimate?" I said, trying to be my debonair self. "'I'm sorry'?"

She wrinkled her full mouth. "As if I hadn't heard that one a million times before," she sniffed.

Randi chided me with her eyes. One for Sari's side, zilch for mine. The sparks I was setting off at the outset weren't exactly celebratory.

I struggled for a comeback. "I hope we won't step on each other's toes."

"I'll be sure to let you know if you do," she snapped. "We both have to work hand and have to be fair to all parties." That last part sounded grudgingly obligatory. She clearly didn't hold our profession in awe. Her bristly attitude may have been instinctively defensive, given her own job and knowing she wasn't likely to please anybody here. She needed someone to smooth those ruffled feathers of hers.

Enter my trusty sidekick. "After all," Randi piped up brightly, "if we uncover the diamond soon, your company wins—and so do the Huntingtons."

One of her darkly beautiful eyes widened. "You have some prospects already?"

"We've just started," I offered, "but I think we're good at what we do."

"Wait a minute. Christmas, Christmas Agency." She tried crinkling the shiny dark skin of her forehead and fortunately didn't do a very good job, too young to have developed the veteran wrinkles I brought so eminently to the fore. "Aren't you the ones who couldn't save that kidnapped scientist last month?"

Of course that's what we'd wanted everyone to think, so I couldn't deny it, giving her a reluctant nod. "Maybe not our most shining moment," I admitted, "but we did solve the mystery—sort of." I had to let her know we had still achieved a victory of sorts, however pyrrhic. She needn't know the resolution wasn't the same everyone else had drawn.

No response but the wry tilt of her mouth showed that healthy sense of skepticism so necessary in her line of work and mine. I felt a professional bond developing, however tenuous—though she apparently didn't feel the same way since she shook her head as she slung her valise up the stairs to the front door. Well, Descartes did warn the world during the Age of Reason, doubt everything. I didn't think it healthy to share that little nugget with her right then.

I offered to help her at least with her baggage but she shrugged me off. "Just my laptop. A tool of the trade these days."

"We each have our own special tools," I said, slapping my chest where I hoped my gun bulged enough to impress her. That left me with only my tongue which I shouldn't have flapped open so freely, though, before I realized I should have put that differently to someone of her gender. Randi had placed her weapon in a place not quite so strategically located for her to show off her strength as I'd tried to. She had definitely put a decidedly distaff touch on the idea of a concealed weapon to keep our witnesses on their best behavior. I had a feeling she was ahead of the game, at least in the deception department. I was pretty sure she had the better showpiece—and more potential panache in her display whenever the time came. Now wasn't it. Wisely, she did nothing except shift her weight from one leg to the other and smile. Good choice.

"Duty calls," I said with a wave as we returned to the van, "but we'll be back."

"I'll alert the media," she said, ringing the doorbell and seeming happy to turn her back on us as Wade opened the door and let her in as if admitting a gust of wind. My gosh! Could it be she was referring to the sardonic line spoken by Sir John Gielgud in his Oscar-winning performance as Dudley Moore's prickly manservant in "Arthur"? Nah, couldn't be. She didn't seem the movie maven type. Too young to know that film anyway.

"Well," said Randi, already a shrewd observer, "that was certainly a cold shoulder if I ever felt one."

"Get used to it."

"It was for you," she pointed out with a smile, "not me. At least she didn't hate me at first sight."

"So you're my in?"

"You better believe it," she crowed, a hand on my shoulder.

But I was musing as we made our way next door in the van. "Don't you think it's odd," I finally said, "that whoever took the diamond didn't try to replace it with a replica? You know, like in the movies? So the theft might not have been noticed for days or weeks."

"Maybe they didn't have time enough to think it through. How often are you going to get a storm to make the theft even easier?"

"The worn wiring to the backup generator seems unusually fortuitous, too."

"Chance and happenstance?" Then she pressed a forefinger thoughtfully to her lips. "Substituting it with a fake would have certainly given the perps more time to skedaddle."

"The obvious benefit," I emphasized.

"Unless they didn't have far to go." She raised that forefinger now in air. "It's almost as if they wanted it known the diamond *had* been taken."

I couldn't resist the Bogie fillip. "Bingo!" I'd already come to that conclusion.

But why?

Had that revelation gotten us any closer to a solution—or only deepened the mystery?

6

The approach to the Hadids' mansion seemed more garish than the Huntingtons' kinder, gentler incline. A wide concrete drive swooped up towards a four-car garage that featured the same orange-tiled roof as the rest of what looked like a modern version of a Middle Eastern stucco palace roosted atop the rise so ostentatiously. The single iron gate at the entrance flanked by tall box elder bushes opened even as we drove up to the intercom, the "H" at its center resembling two scimitars linked by a crossbar that looked like a spear armed at both ends.

Mr. Hadid answered through the speaker personally right away as if anxious for the company, hesitating at first only until I announced who we were and why we were there, then asked us in. "Anything to help find peasant who rob friends. What is world coming to?" He had a clipped, booming way of talking, a foreign accent that made it sound like he was proud to speak English even if he didn't know it all that well.

Parked in front of the imposing porch was a Firebird TransAm, an odd choice that made Randi lean forward agape but had me wondering. Earmarks of the nouveau riche—or pretended wealth? After the real estate balloon burst in 2008 to reveal mortgages too many people should never have qualified for, we couldn't assume anyone was necessarily as well-off as their homes implied, though admittedly the collapse had separated the wheat from the chaff. Which were they? Yet to be seen.

When we entered the foyer, a two-story atrium with an enormous gaudy chandelier overhead, I was glad Randi had worn a dress after all to upstage my corduroy jacket and turtleneck. Mr. Hadid nodded with a sly grin, his ruddy complexion and handsomeness reminding me of Ricardo Montalban. Mrs. Katalena Hadid, swarthy, short and stout, waddled forward in a wide-leg palazzo, flowing pants reminiscent of those harem girls had worn in movies, flouting a long veil-like scarf at her neck which drew some attention away from lipstick far too scarlet and maybe hiding wrinkles and possibly a wattle. She looked Randi up and down with an uncertain smile, presumably at the shortness of her skirt while also admiring the style. No such uncertainty from Vincent Hadid, of course, who brightened at her appearance as if it were an invitation. We already knew their first names from Peter but went through the formalities.

"Would you like some coffee?" said Mrs. Hadid politely. "I have knafeh just out of oven."

Randi looked at me, a barely concealed plaintive look that only I recognized for what it was, but then asked Mrs. Hadid, "What's 'knafeh'?"

"Kind of cheese pie—like what you call 'Danish'?"

"We don't mean to stay long," I inserted, "but if it's no bother—" It was an easy way out for us either way.

"We have coffee now anyway," she explained, "so no bother. The nanny take children to park to play the soccer so is just us." Her dark eyes flicked towards Vincent. She had a full face, plump and pitted with acne scars, those flowing pants an effort to minimize her girth. She seemed with that glance to think she didn't deserve someone as good-looking as Vincent. And in fact with her iron-gray hair and squat stature, she looked more like Vincent's mother than his wife. Vincent swept a palm back over his temple flecked with white making him look even more cosmopolitan.

She seemed almost robotic in her serving mode, already turning to prepare a tray for us.

"How is it you came to make friends with the Huntingtons?" I started out maybe a little too bluntly.

"They greet us with fruit basket when we first move in new house," said Victor after insisting we call him that. He sprawled in a Naugahyde easy chair, crossing a long leg over his thigh as he lounged back, gesturing for me to sit opposite in the white sofa. Seeing that our hostess was assuming the domestic duties so readily, Randi pitched in accompanying Mrs. Hadid to the galley kitchen and helped her prepare the servings as a courtesy to the graciousness of our hostess that made her smile back a little self-consciously as if she didn't merit such attention. "We, as you say, just hit it off," Vincent went on. "'Hit.' I get kick out of this English!" The "this" sounded more like "these."

Randi placed the tray of cups and the silver pot on the ornate coffee table, making room for Lena's platter, as he was calling her now, who set the knafeh down beside it. They smelled wonderfully of orange before she plopped into a straight-backed chair with an audible "Ooomph" and Randi took her place beside me, a hand on my forearm.

"That's some car you've got out there," I said.

"The old lady," he said with a broad smile, "let me buy. She the money bags."

Lena scowled at him but added, "My family from Massachusetts in clothing business. I am seamstress still for—" She gestured by rubbing her thumb across her fingers. "—the pin money as you say."

"Firebird not car professor buy," said Vincent, "but flashy and fast."

"'Professor'?"

"I teach the Spanish at Pacific U in Forest Grove," he said, rolling his "r's" mellifluously so that the town sounded classier than its farming origins belied, "and Arabic at Portland State. Not retired like our friends. But what is this our nice neighbor lose? You not say."

The Hadids didn't know anything about the crime when they'd left. Mention of it would have been revealing. They seemed sincerely in the dark until I told them.

"So many pretty things they have," said Lena, rolling her own diamond ring around her pudgy finger, apparently so we wouldn't notice how small it was. "We have only this—race car." She said it as if she were about to spit. "Vincent likes too much the dogs."

I paled at the way she said that since she didn't recognize the double meaning. Dead silence fell between us like a guillotine. Fortunately, they didn't get it. Vincent scowled a moment, then turned to us with a strained but wide smile. "I have method." As every gambler did, I thought. "So I win sometime."

"Sometime," Lena harrumphed.

Vincent ignored her tone. "You have suspects?"

"A work in progress," I repeated, a phrase I had taken on lately like a reluctant mantra. I looked around seeing how neatly arranged everything was, even the satiny pillows on the sectional sofa curving about the fireplace that looked like she never let anyone use it. "Your children were home by themselves that night?"

"With Hanna but they old enough to trust," said Lena, sticking out her substantial if quite drooping chest.

"Tye and Siva teenager," Vincent added more tentatively, "but Hanna good for."

I heard Randi bite into the dessert and make an "ummm" sound, closing her eyes before sharing a glance my way for me to try it before she sipped her very thick black coffee.

"When will they be getting back?" I said.

Lena looked at the cuckoo clock which had just tolled eleven. "For the lunch."

"We'd like to talk with Hanna later," I said.

"You come back then?" said Lena expectantly.

We nodded. "Just to verify details," I added.

On our way out, Randi turned to me before getting into her side of the van. "They don't seem likely prospects, do they?"

I shrugged. "He does gamble. That means debts."

"But she's 'money bags.' She doesn't seem to know when to say no to him."

"What she doesn't know," I said with raised eyebrows, "could hurt them both."

"So what do we do in the meantime before seeing about Hanna and the children?"

"I think we should revisit our client and then her husband," I said.

"Together?"

"Better apart. Divide—to conquer."

"My feelings exactly."

"By dropping by unannounced at their workplaces."

"To throw them off?"

I grinned. She was getting the hang of this. "Sometimes that reaps better results."

"'Reaps,'" she giggled. "You make it sound deliciously dangerous."

"PI privilege?"

"More like typically Nicky." She was getting to know me too well.

We started with "Lord" Matthew Vandemere first, since he was closer at a downtown Ashborough branch. His bank was rumored to be closing in its local consolidation efforts to save money. We already knew "Lord Matt" had had to settle for his precarious position there because of an economy faltering under Bush II's cavalier indifference during his reign that encouraged rampant industry greed. So he was likely living on the edge, knowing he might soon be cut.

I scanned the small parking lot when we took our place in one of the diagonal slots looking for a car that might be his, until we noticed the red Shelby. They must be sharing the vehicle to save money. Randi nodded at our playing that speculation game. He'd dropped his wife off first.

It was almost noon when we asked a teller if we could see the loan officer, a Mr. Matthew Vandemere, knowing too well titles here didn't count. I gave her my card.

"He's the *assistant* loan officer," corrected the dark-complexioned girl whose name badge announced her as Mandie. Well, maybe *that* title did.

I cast a knowing side-glance at my sidekick who secretly elbowed my rib. She knew.

Mandie scratched at a high-boned cheek, bright eyes flitting from me to Randi in what I took to be wonderment rather than awe. Our profession commanded respect only to the TV generation, but at least she seemed an active member in her spare time. We were glad to cash in on it where we could, even if here it didn't matter much. "Does he know what this is about?"

"He should," I affirmed.

"I'll make sure he isn't too busy."

But we could see for ourselves as she went to the south side of the small building, sectioned off by plexiglass half-walls that made it look like a transparent rat maze. A man at a large computer monitor flagged with myriad post-it notes looked up at Mandie, startled, but instantly bounded up from the office chair like a jack-in-the-box, pulled down his suit jacket and adjusted the perfect Windsor knot of his black tie, his prominent Adam's apple bobbing as he walked warily towards us, glowering at the card, then cocking his head at us. It was like watching a prisoner on the other side of a plastic baffle during visiting hours.

"Come back to my private office," he said, his hand not touching but coaxing us into a dead end to the labyrinth. The furthest cubicle looked more like a shared conference area with its empty table than "his office." His lips curled. "Did my wife put you up to this?"

We weren't sure how to interpret that. "You know that she hired us, right?" I said.

He interrupted me with a finger to his puckered lips and hissing with a quick shake of his head, looking around to make sure his colleagues couldn't overhear. How could anyone ever think that half-walls of plexiglass an office makes? I guess no matter where we find ourselves, we tend to reimagine our dungeons as castles.

"Why did you have to come here of all places during working hours yet?" he snarled. "We want this resolved on the Q.T. as quickly as possible."

"She obviously has her parent's blessing to do this," I said. "Is anything wrong with either of them that they can't handle their own finances?"

"Wade is having some memory problems, though nothing serious just yet," said Matthew, the name he wanted us to call him, though he insisted on addressing us more formally. "He asked Mena whether she could take care of their bills since Adeline had written checks on an expired account that bounced. Mena was happy to help since they haven't always been on the best of terms especially since we got married—though I think it goes back further than that."

"They weren't impressed with her marrying a 'Lord'?" I said a bit puckishly.

Despite his sallow complexion worsened by a persistent five o'clock shadow, he reddened at his neck as he again looked around to make sure no one had heard that either. He leaned forward towards us, clasping his hands together and lowering his voice. "It's just a hereditary title from my father who's from Germany originally. I mean, no castles or hidden fortune or anything like that. But it did technically make Mena a 'Lady.' I'm still proud of the heritage, though it's nothing we can make use of hereabouts."

"Certainly not in these social circles," said Randi.

"Some people in high places are still impressed, Miss Degrotti—like at the Women's Auxiliary Garden Club, which Mena belongs to. Wives of doctors and lawyers and such."

"Are things still touch-and-go with you and your in-laws," I said, looking for a reason for the discord, "because you both settled for jobs like this?"

"I *was* hoping for a better position after the time I've invested here," said Matthew, a finger working at the collar where his tie was knotted. "They wanted their daughter to 'marry well.' I don't think I made that cut, title or not. At least not yet."

I burrowed on. "Have you or your wife ever handled anything dealing with their collection before?"

Matthew drummed his fingers at the glossy, mostly empty desktop. "They're mostly just expensive memorabilia. He built up quite a nest egg and now has something to show for it."

"With your wife the sole heir?" I added.

He narrowed his eyes. "That's—kind of up in the air."

"And you have no children of your own?" said Randi.

"We hope to," he said, "but right now we need the two incomes."

"So you're planning on them?" she persisted.

"If Mena can have them, yes," he said. "She's had—some problems in the past."

I picked up the baton. "Problems?"

"A miscarriage," he said, eyes darkening, "the first year we were married. But we've gotten past that and she's taking the pill until the time is ripe." He was fidgeting now. "I'm not sure this is the time or place for such personal questions. I'm on the company clock here. And they're always watching."

"Sorry," I said. "We just thought we should introduce ourselves and assure you we're doing what we can to find the missing item."

He got up, sighing again. "Thanks for that, I guess. We have to keep this hush-hush. My wife chose your agency for that very reason." He ventured a tentative smile as he shook our hands again.

"We'll keep you both in the loop," I said as Randi

hoisted up her capacious purse. But I turned before leaving that plexiglass cell of his. “Oh, and by the way, could we bother you for your bank records? I presume they’re here?”

He stopped in his tracks, jerking his angular jaw back. “Why would you need that?”

I looked at Randi who returned the glance with a glimmer of a smile, knowing why I was rocking the boat. But Randi came to my defense with my own previous defense. “Standard procedure,” she said though it wasn’t always.

“She’s paying you out of her parents’ account. You know they’re good for it.”

“We like to be thorough,” I said.

He shook his head with obvious impatience. “Mena takes care of all our personal banking.”

“With you in a position like this?” Randi broke back in.

“I get too much of it here at Oregon National,” he said under his breath. “She actually enjoys balancing the checkbook. For me it would be like a busman’s holiday. I’d much rather watch the Mariners or tinker in the garage when I can.” Although sweat was dripping down his temples, he ventured a half-smile as if I could relate to that, though I couldn’t imagine him ignoring a looker like his wife even if she had come across as more than a little stand-offish. After all, it was still just the two of them at home.

“We’ll get the info from your wife then,” I said.

“You’re going off to talk with her now?”

“We said we’d keep her updated. Routine really.” I didn’t want to show our hand yet or he might forewarn her we’d be dropping in at her office next.

"I see," he said uncertainly.

"You've got our card if you need to share anything else," I added.

He looked back at his desk as if that were his safety zone. In a way it was. "Okay," he muttered.

"Au revoir!" I said probably a bit more gaily than the situation warranted, letting him know we'd see him again—sometime. Through the windows as we walked out to the parking lot, I glanced back to his plastic prison to see if he were reaching for his cell phone but he still looked like he'd been hit by a truck.

"Very clever, Mr. Christmas," she said, when we climbed into the van. "Rattling the cage to see what falls out. I like the way you ran the show there."

"You'll get your chance to play first string," I said.

"I better," she smirked. "You act as if everyone's guilty."

"That's because," I said, as I tried to ease into the traffic already thickening with the noon glut, "everyone is—of something."

She eyed me askance. "You think that even of your own partner?"

"You prefer staying a little mysterious sometimes."

"Keeps you interested, doesn't it?"

I chuckled. "Everybody loves a mystery? But only for so long. We have to know what's behind it all in the end."

"Like a diamond?"

"Is that what you're hiding, too?"

She pinched her lips together playfully. "Diamonds come in all shapes and sizes."

"I don't think our thieves believe that for a minute!"

7

Mena worked on the east side of town in nearby Orenco Station rather than downtown like Matthew. The Evermore Title Company was tucked into a strip mall decorated with brick that gave it a false sense of permanence, the truth evident in many of the vacancies, an unfortunate sign of the times lingering after a major recession. But we hoped to catch her during the lunch hour—the operative word there being "catch." For that we had to skip lunch ourselves.

"Oh, Nicky!" she complained, a hand at her stomach which had already grumbled its displeasure. "I should have brought along some of my healthy snacks!"

"Sorry, sweetie," I said. "I'll make it up to you."

"Where have I heard that before?"

"Maybe an empty stomach will help us stay alert for red flags."

"We don't have enough already?"

I cast a quick glance her way despite the summer traffic which was fraying my nerves. Apparently the first thing students out of school wanted to do was drive anywhere they could to drive drivers crazier than their teachers.

We were lucky this time to stumble onto Mena the minute we walked through the door. She was conferring with the receptionist about something when she looked up and gaped at us, blinking quickly, turning away from the young red-headed girl in a light green pants suit to sputter out the side of her mouth, "What are *you* two doing here? I'm *working!*"

"We were in the area," I said as innocently as I could, "and just thought we'd stop in to bring you up to speed."

"This is—a private matter," she stammered.

"It's your lunch hour, isn't it?" I said innocently.

Her eyes flicked to the stylized analog modern-art clock with no numbers on it beside the receptionist's desk. However art deco it might be, wasn't that sending a curious subconscious message to workers and customers alike? She tried to clear her throat. "I guess we could grab a cup of coffee at the Starbucks opposite the Pub and Grill."

"The one on the corner?" I'd seen it entering the narrow street leading to the subdivision to the north supposedly discouraging car traffic, but which just made it doubly difficult to navigate. Hard to break ingrained habits like driving cars everywhere in America, a doomed hope for much too optimistic urban planners. It looked pretty crowded.

"If you don't mind waiting," she said, "'crowded' also means more 'private.'"

She moved a token on the "IN/OUT" board at the receptionist's desk as she led us out the front door. I nodded back at the receptionist she'd been talking to whose nameplate read, Monica Delaney. "What do you call her for short in a workplace like this?" I tried to joke. "'Monie'?"

Mena clucked noisily. "Always with the wisecracks. This is serious business, Nick."

"Levity relieves tension," I shrugged with a smirk.

Randi was trying to stifle a giggle with a hand at her mouth.

"Clients would be disappointed," I countered, "if I didn't live up to the PI stereotype."

"Not me," Mena snapped back.

"You definitely need a cup of coffee," I said, undeterred.

She just shook her head glumly. "I can't imagine you have anything instructive to say this soon. I mean, you just met my folks this morning, for God's sakes."

We milled about with the millions crammed into the tiny Starbucks shop lining up in a sinuous mass behind a counter with attendants far cheerier than their edgier patrons growing even edgier. The noise factor made it a little hard to hear but Mena was dead right. Everyone despite the din of the throng was nonetheless lost in his or her own world with or without someone. It had indeed, sadly, become the 21st century's version of privacy.

While we waited and waited—and waited, I said, "We understand from your husband that you take care of the finances in your family."

She flinched, then glowered at us. "You talked with

Matt?"

"We wanted to make sure we were on the same page with you both," I said to make it sound reasonable.

"Well, he doesn't know anything much about anything," she sneered. Her latte couldn't come soon enough.

"He seems to have every confidence in you," I countered.

"I really do have more of a head for business than he does."

We looked amazed, not so much at the statement which might have been true but the attitude towards her one-and-only. Maybe her parents had good reason to distrust her choice.

I had to take the next step. "Then you wouldn't mind sharing your bank account information with us?"

The cords in her neck tightened. "Why would you want that?"

I tried the same tack as earlier. "Background checks are part of the job."

"Well," she said, "I don't see why. We're the ones who asked you to help my folks. We want you to solve the mystery as much as they do."

Randi entered in again, blinking wide-eyed. "You know we're on your side, so you shouldn't mind. We have to make sure this theft isn't a vendetta against you for some debt you or your husband may have or an old grudge against either you or your parents." I was proud of Randi for coming up with that one. Maybe her loving mystery stories helped after all.

Mena visibly softened. "We try to keep up on our bills—and get along fine with people in the community."

"That's what everybody thinks," Randi replied with surprising aplomb.

We had actually gained some ground in the line and were at least within spitting range of one of the baristas, a large busty young woman with what looked like an Indian tilak on her forehead, apparently marking her third eye which she could certainly use to stay ahead of her orders.

"You hired us to protect you, too, as well as your folks," I said, getting in on the act.

She heaved a sigh. "I guess I can give you our account numbers and my password that you have to give the clerk in person."

"Remember," I said, offering her my best Clark Gable smile, "you always have our confidence."

"I made it!" said Randi who had forged ahead like the good scout she is. "What do you guys want? Quick before I lose my lead!" She relayed our orders to the flighty barista acting oblivious to the chaos this crowd posed. Grace under pressure in a barista? Would wonders never cease?

Randi then surprised the both of us by whipping out a Starbucks gift card to foot the bill. So she had her weaknesses, too, with fast food of a slightly loftier kind. A fellow coffee connoisseur to boot. I really *had* won the lottery—or as close as I would ever get.

"Maybe," I quipped, "this will give us the boost we all need."

"I guess," said Mena, "I *could* use something."

We had to continue standing to pick up our orders, then continued standing waiting for one of the tiny tables to vacate, ending up sitting at the "bar" staring out the windows at more traffic on Cornell sluggishly passing by, a scenic display becoming a new standard that beggared belief. No wonder nostalgia had assumed even greater appeal these days.

We did update her on our other visits thus far though I think she seemed fixated more on that last one we'd made to her husband. She spooned at her skinny latte, starting with the foam first before sipping prior to giving us the information we needed that Randi duly entered into her iphone. As we prepared to go, she said, "Sounds like you haven't gotten very far."

"Breakthroughs are often lurking where you're looking but just don't see yet," I granted.

Randi grinned at my Chinese fortune cookie routine but the comment seemed to placate Mena for the moment, even though it was essentially doubletalk, more useful than people realized. She didn't really seem to be listening, though.

Despite the tense tenor of that meeting, we'd learned a few things about our client's character—though we were about to find out more than we wanted.

8

Before returning to the office, I wanted to wrap up our fieldwork for the day by stopping in again at the Hadids, as promised, to check with their nanny Hanna about the children that might reveal more than she might have realized at the time. She had a lovely Swedish accent and, despite her age which I guessed exceeded mine, wore her taffy-colored hair in Heidi-like braids dangling over hunched shoulders that looked like they carried the world.

"I was too busy with the kids," she said, lending the words a sing-song quality ending with an upswing in her voice that made the answer sound like a question.

"They never slipped outside to play then?" I said, making sure they hadn't indulged in any hijinks she may not have been aware of if they scampered off elsewhere.

"I make them snickerdoodles to dunk in their chocolate milk."

"And they went right to bed before the Hadids came back?" Randi added.

"They snuggle in quilts I make," she said. "Puts them right to sleep, ya?"

"And the Hadids when they got home?" I said. "Nothing unusual there either?"

"I was asleep myself in what they call the granny unit near them—though they make the noises." She looked around to make sure no one could hear us. "I don't like to say but the Missus, she snores like the buzz saw. And the Mister, he laughs from way down here inside, you know at everything?" She gestured by holding her considerable belly. "I sleep not so good since my Gunnar die."

Randi tilted her head. "Mr. Hadid was still laughing when he came back?"

"I think so," she said, leaving out the "h" in "think" but trying not to. "He laughs lots with other people, her not so much. She has the sour look more."

Randi and I both gazed around. We'd seen Lena in the kitchen before taking Hanna aside, but not Vincent. "Where's 'Mister Victor' now?" Randi said.

"He go out much," she said, "in that noisy car."

Afterwards when we got back in the van, Randi said, "Victor sure sounds like something else."

"Something else entirely than what his wife thinks," I grinned back. She'd sensed what I had, too, that he was something of a gadabout, to put it euphemistically.

Agreeing to settle for "take out" from The Grinder across the street for now to tide us over, I set her to work on the computer that afternoon at the office scouring the Vandemere's bank records since Mena had given us her password for that, too.

"Interesting password, 'rabbit hole,'" she muttered.

"Who doesn't love *Alice in Wonderland*?" I said.

I was admiring just as much, though, the way her thin fingers and those fascinating pink fingernail extensions flew over the keyboard so nimbly, making a mesmerizing clickety -clack with their tapping.

"How can you type so fast with such long nails?"

"You get used to it like they're not there," she said over her shoulder. "But I'm glad you noticed!"

"How could I not?"

"That's the whole idea," she teased.

She printed out transactions for the last six months for the file we were starting on this case. A couple of deposits caught our attention within the last couple of months, one for $20,000, another for $50,000, the latter from her parents, though we couldn't readily identify the source for the former. We'd have to check with the bank for the donor. Mena had also provided her birthdate and secret word, "Mattster," for us to use at the bank if necessary, the latter suggesting she might still harbor some left-handed respect for her husband after all. People were nothing if not constant contradictions. I could see why Randi liked to while away her spare time with crossword puzzles. Answers there were either right or wrong, not like real-life.

When we were done poring over the data, me pinching the indentations my reading glasses I'd grudgingly resorted to left on the upper bridge of my nose, I saw Randi yawn and knew we'd had a long day.

That's when the phone bleated, startling the both of us. It was just before five, the end of the workday.

"Time to play receptionist," I said, pointing.

She glared up at the Tweety Bird clock she'd gifted me at the end of the last case as a kind of in-joke since I'd likened her to the cartoon character, me being the cat Sylvester—though I often wondered since then whether I hadn't gotten the roles wrong. "I hate these Last-Minute Larrys—especially when I'm hungry for more than just that half a turkey on rye I never got time to finish."

"A dime is a dime," I said in defense of another possible client or lead.

After a quick sigh, she relented, answering the phone with her pained Happy Hanna face, as she called it. Then she sat upright, rather than slouching as she had at first, preparing to get up and leave when the hour hand hit five. "Oh, hi, Mr. Huntington," she said. "I mean, Wade." A long pause as worry knotted her forehead and she fingered blonde strands back over an ear. "You want us to come over?" She nodded, looking at me for an approving nod which I gave her. "Okay."

I turned off my computer as she hung up. "What's wrong?"

"His wife's sick." She picked up her purse which, looking almost half her size, could have contained a kitchen sink from the way she hefted it to her shoulder. "He thinks we should go over that list of people he gave us again for the two who never even RSVP'd." She raised that finger up with a heavy sigh. "And the adjuster called to say she's stopping in with her printed estimate. He thinks we should be there for that anyway."

I plied my lower lip with a finger. "The only thing she had to do was determine today's market value." I paused. "I wonder if that's why his wife isn't well, worried sick over what the girl's going to say." But I stared at her. She had the mottled cheeks that told me just how tired she was, though to me she looked even prettier like this, a halo-like glow suffusing her face. "You sure you're up to this?"

"I'm getting my second wind." The long breath she exhaled my way smelled pleasantly of licorice from the pellets of Good and Plenty she kept in her desk drawer that I now knew from our hospital stay to be one of her favorite candies. But I sensed a hint of her perfume and maybe the scent of a rose petal, coming, I think, from remnants of the pink lipstick now flecked there. "We need to check on Addy, regardless."

"I know." I could tell despite her bravado she needed even more of an incentive. "I know this is a lot to ask. I'll somehow make it worth your while." I raised two fingers. "Scouts honor."

"Really, Nicky? Nobody says that anymore!"

"That's just me again—not following the ways of the world."

She paused, returning a tired smirk. "You're really offering me a carrot at the end of the stick for giving you more than a hundred percent today?"

I wasn't about to call attention to another accidental double entendre. "More than just pizza and champagne."

She tilted her head, hair whispering over her shoulder. "You're a crafty one, Nicky, knowing the art of keeping me dangling all the time—dang it!"

So we were off again, hopeful to net more leads than dead ends, arriving back at the Huntingtons half an hour later.

Despite this being late in the afternoon and typically the hottest time of the day, Sari was waiting in her car with the windows rolled down in the shade of the manor clacking at her laptop when we pulled up behind her. I saw her notice us in her rearview mirror so I sidled up beside her and said, "I'm glad we caught you."

"If I'm all you've caught today," she mocked, "you're fishing in the wrong hole."

"We're narrowing it down," I joked back. It was all I could muster this late in the day.

She clicked the right key. Something churned out of her mini-printer with the sound of a toy truck. "I'll meet you inside with the results where it's more comfortable."

"We stopped by," said Randi, hands on the window sticking up slightly from the driver's side of her Escort like a thin blade, "because we understand Mrs. Huntington is feeling under the weather."

"She looked pale," admitted Sari, looking down at the paper emerging like a dark tongue, "when I left earlier."

"We'll see you in a minute then?" Randi added. She could charm a beast—but not this one.

Wade Huntington was already standing at the doorway to welcome us with a grim smile, now sporting a velvet burgundy smoking jacket filigreed with countless fleur di lis crosses, the kind Hugh Hefner used to wear although it somehow didn't seem as anachronistic on Wade.

"What's gone wrong?" Randi reached out for his forearm as he backed away, not so much from her touch as to let us in again, though he also seemed pleasantly surprised by her concern. She didn't let go for a long moment.

"She turned worse after lunch," he said, his voice cracking.

"Was it something you ate then?" Randi asked.

"Maria made us some roast beef sandwiches—but I had the same thing and I'm okay."

"It could be a late spring bug," Randi offered though her face said she didn't think it could be that simple.

"She *has* been awfully worried about the theft, feeling like we were, I don't know, violated somehow," said Wade. "And now with this appraisal pending—" He looked down as he led us into the kitchen where Maria was preparing salmon filets on a vented baking sheet.

Randi leaned towards him. "May we see her?"

He shook his head slowly once. "Not yet. She's been napping most of the afternoon."

"Have you called the doctor?" I said.

"She didn't want me to," Wade answered, "hoping she'll get better on her own. She wants to wait and see how she is tomorrow."

Maria came over to him with a cocktail glass of a deep

golden liquid I took to be bourbon. "Ah," he said lighting up somewhat, "whiskey really *is* 'the water of life.' Our distant ancestors certainly knew the value of liquor over gems." He looked up at Maria. "Would you offer some to our guests?"

I looked at my watch, considering a number of factors here. "It *is* after office hours," I said. "Maybe just one for the road?"

He wrinkled his lips into a hesitant smile. "Can you say that now in your line of work?"

"I don't always go with the grain," I grinned, glancing at Randi to indicate I thought it would help him feel we were more friends right now than detectives.

Randi jumped in, volunteering. "I wouldn't mind being the designated driver if you don't mind delaying my reward."

"More brownie points?" I said.

"I'm building up quite a cache to cash in on," she riposted, more on the ball this late in the day than I was, delighting in the double-duty homonym. Maybe she really *had* gotten her second wind. I only hoped it was contagious.

I shared a glance with Wade whose eyes now twinkled as he looked at Randi, then me, registering more than that idle banter. "She certainly is a breath of fresh air," he breathed out. I'm sure those first few sips of bourbon had already helped him deal with his wife's downturn—but the real anodyne here, as anyone could see, was Randi.

Maria served me a similar drink that I diluted with a splash of soda from the crystal dispenser she kindly presented on a silver tray.

Wade rolled his shoulders forward at my acceptance. With him more relaxed, I took out our copy of the list from my breast pocket and asked, "You said a couple of guests never RSVP'd?"

Just then, though, the front door eased open the way a burglar might sneak in. Wade hadn't shut it all the way. Sari's very small feet seemed to rattle around in those clunky storm-trooper boots making her lean forward slightly as if she might topple, Tinker Bell in Frankenstein elevator shoes.

She clutched the print-outs like a sheaf of wheat she wanted to strangle, her drawn almond eyes more like the slits for the eyes of Klatu, the giant robot from "The Day the World Stood Still."

"Would you—" Wade offered, a hand indicating the tray with the decanter of bourbon.

She waved the thought away as if batting at a fly. "No, thanks. I'm still on company time. I wanted to say this is a tentative estimate, Mr. Huntington. A reviewer has to approve my report and file another report for my supervisor before it'll be official. And there'll be a waiting period of a month to see if Mr. Christmas's agency turns up the diamond before a check can be cut." She made that sound ominous, not hard to do with a voice like hers.

"I understand," he nodded, lips thin, the bourbon not quite working all its charms yet.

She offered the sheets to Wade after trying to smooth out the curled pages, then patted her windbreaker jacket that made a papery rattle on an inside pocket. "This appraisal that Christie's had from Harry Winston mentions the possibility that the diamond's gold color may have been artificially enhanced by radiation."

"There's some controversy about the gold hue, that's true," he said, "but we figured it was still worth a gamble because of its remarkable beauty, as Addy kept reminding me—and of course its historical significance."

"So you bought it ten years ago," she said through pinched lips, "for five million."

He crooked a smile. "I'd say we got a steal, cashing in on that dispute. It's probably worth at least double that, maybe more because of its provenance and rich legends. The Maharajah Singh is said to have secured his reign with it at the turn of the 19th century." He was obviously repeating that for her benefit.

"You must understand my dilemma then," she explained. "I have to protect your interests because you've been a good policy holder all these years—but also my firm's."

He examined the summary of salient facts cover of her report, then sat up straighter. "You're only vouchsafing it for five million??"

"It's what you paid for it," she said. "A bill of sale is the best evidence of value."

"But ten years ago?" he blurted. "It's got to be worth more than that just from simple appreciation."

"Possibly," she granted with a half nod. "But we don't deal in speculative value."

Wade gritted his teeth as he ran a finger beneath his flared nostrils. "I can't share this with Addy just now. She's too weak."

Both of them looked at me, then Randi who had eased back into a chair at the bar where Maria favored her with a cup of tea instead.

"We'd rather leave it in your capable hands, Nick," Wade said, forehead creased, "and just get the damned thing back intact."

"So," said Sari, dark eyes flashing, "would we."

"We'll do our best," I reassured them both.

"The trail is still warm," Randi joined in trying to buoy up our spirits though for me the bourbon was doing more than its fair share.

Wade set down the glass on a cork coaster.

"Well," Sari said—who's sorry now? I thought wryly—"I'll be off."

"You couldn't have put it better," I parried.

She glowered at me, then regarded Randi where she apparently hoped to find some gender support—though Randi, bless her heart, avoided giving her that satisfaction by keeping her eyes riveted on me instead with a knowing grin.

"You'll be hearing from us," I added.

"We're banking on it," she bristled and clomped off in those oversized boots as she let the door quietly fall shut. And here I'd half-expected to catch a long high-collared cape flapping in the wind behind her. No such luck.

"I think, Nicky," said Randi, "you've made something of an enemy."

Wade chuckled. "You're not alone."

"We seem to keep hitting the same ceiling as the last

case," Randi said with a resigned half-smile before I could say anything about the list. "Five million was the same ransom Syntek ended up paying for Dr. James, too."

Wade put his two-cents in—worth, of course, more than that. "It must be the going rate today for legal thievery."

The fog of the alcohol had dulled my fear but also galvanized my bravado. I rattled the paper in my hand by hopefully flicking it with a forefinger. "Which are the two guests on this list you said never replied?"

Wade's lips clicked, dark blue eyes darting back and forth, catching the glint of the ice cubes that clinked like lonely jewels in his old-fashioned glass, as he pointed. "The foreign-sounding names there."

The ever-vigilant Maria noticed and nicely refilled his glass without his having to ask. She whispered something in his ear, then turned towards us. "Why not you stay? Miss Addy, she not come down."

"I could use the company," Wade agreed.

"Thanks for the offer," I said, "but I've sort of promised Randi a nice dinner somewhere just the two of us. We both put in a long day."

Randi looked at me, eyes glassy tired but obviously pleased. "Maybe another time though?" she said.

"I'll hold you two to that, you hear?" said Wade, looking up at us from under the ridge of his puffy, snow-white eyebrows.

I mentioned the first of the ones he'd pointed out. "Dr. Kane and Dr. Ava Kaslowski—married or brother and sister?"

"Married," he said. "They're archeology professors at the University of Oregon I met at a charity event last month."

"And Dr. Mikel Arkov and Dr. Sasha Barishnikol?" I said.

"American physicists working for an institution called GEOS. It stands for Global Energy OutSourcing, I think. They expressed interest in the diamond at the same event so we invited them to see it for themselves."

"You heard back from everyone else?"

"Lame excuses all, if you ask me," he said. "Everybody seems wrapped up in their own little worlds. Not the Hadids, though. Frankly, I think they were anxious to get away from their kids."

"Wild?" I said.

"Teenagers!" Wade chuckled as if that explained everything. "We'd figured before the dinner 'party,' if you can call it that after so many no-shows, that we'd probably just bequeath the diamond to the Portland Art Museum along with the rest of our collection. There's a tax advantage to the surviving spouse but it'd also be less of a hassle than risking having someone do God knows what to it in the name of science."

"You don't mind then," I said, "if we contact these people?"

"Help yourself," he shrugged. "We met them only that once though they don't seem the type who'd stoop to stealing." He rubbed at his grizzled chin, clearly not having shaved today.

We'd forgotten one last thing, though, I realized as we

accompanied Wade to see if Addy had awakened yet. I had to ask about that gift of $50,000 to his daughter.

"Oh, that," he said, mildly surprised, I think, that we'd found out about it, then giving a nod, understanding that it was part of our job. "They haven't had an easy time of it, especially now that Matthew might be a casualty in the downsizing. We thought it might help them get on their feet while they're both looking for better employment. And it might make up for not leaving much behind if we donate so much away. I'm not sure they could handle the complications of our other investments anyway." He toyed with his gold wedding ring, its setting also boasting a more modest diamond—two carats maybe? "Better to see them enjoy this gift while we're still alive."

"It wasn't then," I said, "for anything specific?"

"She offered to help get our house in order in her spare time. I'm tired of dealing with everyday finances. That pleased her, I think. We haven't always been on the best of terms lately."

I'll bet, I thought. She might even be able to act like a "real" Lady with some of their holdings at her fingertips. But I forced myself to stay courteous.

"You know anything about that extra twenty grand she also received?" I said.

He rubbed his chin and looked at us, forehead furrowed. "It wasn't from us."

"She doesn't moonlight somewhere else?" Randi interjected.

"No, no," Wade said. "She does flutter around sometimes like a chicken with her head cut off, though. Takes a little after Addy that way. But at least it shows gumption and foresight that she hired you people—and maybe that she really cares about our welfare."

I wasn't sure how to respond to that so just said, "Right"—but drawing out the word.

"We've got to be careful not to assume too much," Randi added, I think to cushion any imprudence on my part, "while we're sorting out the facts."

That was my own cautionary advice coming back to bite me.

But it brought a surprised if weary smile to Wade's face plus a side glance over at me. "You're pretty level-headed, my dear, for one so young. If only my daughter were more like you."

"She does keep me in my place," I said to cushion her cushioning.

Wade led us down to the end of his Hall of Fame and peered in. "She's up," he nodded and let us in. Wearing a quilted pink bed jacket which didn't help her pale complexion any, Addy was trying to watch television in their king-sized bed.

Randi padded over to her side along with Wade and held her hand before he had a chance to. "Feeling better?"

"Not much." Her voice crackled, but more, I think, because her throat sounded dry.

"You don't seem like you're holding up very well," said Wade. "Is chicken broth enough?"

"I'm not sure I can even swallow that much," she rasped.

Randi said, "I'll bring it upstairs if you like."

"That'd be sweet," said Wade. "Maria sometimes tries to do too much."

So Randi did while Wade went back downstairs and I waited for Randi to try to help her drink it down. Then Addy finally shook her head. "No good. Can't swallow."

"You sure you shouldn't go to emergency right now?" said Randi.

"I hate hospitals." But she could barely get the words out.

On our way out, we suggested to Wade that he might have to put his foot down. "Addy can be pretty stubborn sometimes," he said. "She's afraid of doctors."

Randi and I just looked at each other before I said, "We'll check in again tomorrow."

"Probably late in the day, though," I added.

"That'd be nice," he said, looking down guiltily as he finished the bourbon and sat at the table in the nook instead of having Maria serve dinner in the dining room.

I'd had only that one drink but Randi insisted she try driving the van so I let her because I could tell she was really looking out for me. "Just tell me where to go," she said in a measured voice, catching herself, "but be nice!"

I chuckled. "I'd never inflict my sharp tongue on you, sweetie."

"Nicky!" she tittered nervously. "You must be tired. Did you really *hear* what you just said?"

"You know what I meant," I said, though I flushed, not realizing this time myself how else it could have been interpreted. Maybe the bourbon *had* loosened my tongue more than I knew.

When I looked back at the Huntington house from the passenger side, I noticed the lowering sun glanced off the complex roof of gables and hip shingled with burnished steel, making the house appear to glow. "Do you see that in your rearview mirror?" I said to Randi.

She checked the mirror. "It almost looks like the house is staring at us with eyes of fire." Then she yawned while I fought following suit. "We must be punch-drunk with fatigue."

A strange feeling washed over me. Could it mean something else? "I think we need this time away from everything tonight," I said. "It might help freshen our perspective."

"I think you're fresh enough as it is with that glass of bourbon," she smirked. "But I could certainly use some refreshment to catch up with you."

"You deserve it—and then some."

"And you're just the one to give it to me?"

"Now who's targeting whom with an even sharper tongue?"

That reduced both of us to gales of child-like laughter, proof positive that Randi's assessment was too true. Even a temporary respite that night, though, would never prepare us for what we were about to face.

9

I had to hand it to Randi, though. She was certainly learning her way around the block—as if this kind of stealth was second nature to her. It showed in the way she dressed the next day for U.S. Bank where the Vandemeres had their joint account. That Thursday she looked like a long-lost waif to my doting father-like presence, wearing her hair tied back with a white scarf and a modest sky-blue dress with a deceptively conservative Peter Pan collar that flared with a dropped V-waist she identified as Basque outlined even more with a light gold chain. The sexy innocence she exuded was palpable, even more so when she smoothed a hand over the fitted triangular front seam that arrowed down to its deliciously inverted apex, as if men needed direction there. We did in all other respects but certainly not that one!

I flashed my license, of course, but Randi's fluttering eyelashes did more for getting the stocky clerk named Jake to look up who had written that $20,000-check. It obviously helped that we had Mena's account number and her aural password "Mattster," though the word also subtly suggested he might not truly be the master of his own house.

That lent us some psychological cachet, proving we had our client's confidence. The bank had its rules, but we had our wiles. I was delighted now to be armed with Randi's womanly ones at my side as well. I let her have her mischievous way with Jake. She basked in her element while I was wise enough to let her take the reins. That didn't stop the hackles from rising at the back of my neck with the way his marled eyes raked over her figure. It was getting to be a challenge to bite my tongue for the sake of probing for improprieties.

Randi came away from his small alcove of an office into the lobby staring at the copy with a shake of her head. "One of the names on Wade's list just jumped up a notch."

"Who wrote the check?"

"We have yet to identify the fellow's rank there, but the company's insignia and name are unmistakable." She showed me the copy. The logo depicted an Earth for the letter "O" cut in half by a bolt of lightning. GEOS.

"I guess we'd better have a talk with 'Boris' and 'Natasha' first off," I said.

She crooked her head. "You're having me on again, aren't you? That's not really their first names."

"I can't fool you," I teased.

"So what's the backstory?"

"The names are from a TV cartoon series called 'The Rocky and Bullwinkle Show' from my father's day," I said.

"Ah," she giggled. "The classics then."

"Where would America be without its comics?" I came back.

"Those GEOS scientists," she said, her forehead knotted, "are more serious about that diamond than Wade realizes. But twenty grand? Isn't that a piddly amount considering an institute like that wants dibs on the diamond?"

"It must be a down payment on something more, but what are they supposed to do to earn the rest? The mind reels!"

"I have a feeling," she said with a raised eyebrow, "we're about to find out—not so much what these scientists say but how they act when we show up. Body language tells us more than words, right?"

I looked at the way she cocked her hip and swaggered out to the car, then chuckled. "As the poet says, 'A little learning *is* a dangerous thing.'"

She cast a saucy glance over her shoulder. "What can I say? I'm a fast learner."

"The sign of a good teacher is when he starts learning more from his protégé," I laughed. "Now let's visit our Russian researchers."

GEOS occupied a sprawling complex of steel and green-tinted glass buildings next to a wildlife sanctuary along Rock Creek in the nearby suburb of Beaverton on a large tract of rolling hills. An island reluctant to become part of the Beaverton suburb, it was almost a city unto itself with its own sewer treatment plant and field of solar energy screens that looked like an array of tilted chessboard squares. Because it spanned so much acreage, it took us a while to wend our way through the traffic on Jenkins Road that marked its southern boundary before we could turn into a vast parking lot in front of what loomed like its own city of Oz.

"Wow," she said. "I think I'd better change into something classier than this little girl lost outfit."

I stared at her and down at the purse by her feet. "Don't tell me that luggage you call a purse is a magic hat."

"Sort of," she laughed. "I didn't know what we were going to do today so I brought along a change of clothes like I've done before. Riding shotgun with you has more riders attached than you ever let on."

"A female Sherlock Holmes with all your costumes *and* a much prettier Gaby Hayes all rolled into one? How could I be so lucky?"

She rolled her eyes. "Whoever that last guy was!"

"You don't know Roy Rogers' famous sidekick?"

"You've just made sure I do now. But I'll bet I've got a few more curves to toss around than that Gaby character ever did."

I swallowed noisily. "No question there."

"You always come wearing the same ol' same ol'. Girls need to blend in with their surroundings."

"Will I recognize you when you're done?"

"Barely!" she laughed. "This is a more professional get-up."

"'Professional' how?" I gulped. "You were content with

the clothes you already had on last night when I took you out for our dinner date at Stanford's."

"You kind of caught me with my pants down there," she joked before she shot a hand to her mouth and her face colored.

"I guess we're both tripping over our tongues lately," I chuckled.

"You know what I mean. I didn't know the place was going to be so nice or I would have made you took me back to my apartment first so I could put on an evening dress." Then she paused. "Hey, wait a minute. We were on a 'date'?"

I blanched. I didn't want to make things awkward. I fell back on her own phrase. "You know what I mean."

She hesitated a little longer while I weaved through the traffic searching for the turn-off. "You'll have to forgive me, Nicky, but I'll try to make this quick." She took off the garter holster and slipped it with the gun into the cubby hole as if it were a precious jewel itself.

"That we have to do anyway," I said, "because of the electronic gates." I'd have to keep my metal keepsakes there, too, besides my own gun.

Her lips clicked as she looked shyly over at me. "There's more, I'm afraid. I have to change here in the front. We can't exactly stop the van by the side of this busy road so I can get into the backseat. That would arouse too much attention."

"'Arouse'," I repeated, "being the key word."

"Just please try not to peek, okay?"

"I'll keep my eyes peeled for the turnoff," I squawked.

"You sound funny, Nicky. Do you need some water or something?"

I coughed. "I'll manage."

She unfastened her seat belt and leaned forward to reach behind and unzip the dress. "Eyes front, remember." Then she pulled the dress up over her head, tossing her hair afterwards to straighten it with a gesture that was unintentionally alluring.

I realized just how sharp my peripheral vision really was. I choked out, "*Pink?*"

"Hey! You're not supposed to be looking!" Then she extracted the carefully folded blouse and skirt from her purse and fluttered them out (like a red flag?), apparently to erase invisible creases I wouldn't have noticed anyway. "Underwear has to match what I wear outside."

"Who's going to notice?" I said hoarsely.

"Me, silly!" she said. "But look. You just did!"

"Accidentally," I said, my voice like sandpaper.

"On purpose?"

I paused, trying in vain to focus on the traffic that had let up some as I slowed to exit. I was still afraid someone might pass and see what wasn't very private right now with my private secretary.

Then, as she wriggled forward to the edge of the seat so she could step into the skirt, I glimpsed a little too much of her backside. Being the trained observer good detectives are, I couldn't stop my reaction to the delicate black script by blurting out, "'*Friday*'?!"

She tittered even as she blushed. "Nicky! You're sure noticing a lot for not noticing!"

"But, Randi, it's *not* Friday."

She turned her head aside, affecting a pique. "Both my 'Thursdays' were dirty." Then she added with a smirk, recovering. "Since you've looked when you weren't supposed to, at least you're not going to forget now that I'm your Friday girl."

"Girl *Friday*," I corrected with a choke. She didn't seem to register how reversing the words made that sound—which of course, for its guilelessness, made it sound even more beguiling.

"Whatever," she said with a flick of her hand. Well, maybe she *did* know. Just how "innocent" was this ingénue of mine anyway?

"But, Randi," I said, "days of the week? Isn't that more what little girls wear?"

"You think after what you've just seen that you weren't supposed to, that I'm too little-girlish?"

Very noisily again, I tried to clear my throat. At least, I was thinking, they hadn't been string bikinis. My God, my heart would have stopped for sure! I wasn't doing so well as it was. Then I couldn't help noticing as she arched her hips to slip into the skirt that the front panels of her bikini panties featured frilly scallops across the top above the taunting "Friday" label on that side, too. Dainty *and* fetching. This "little girl" was a secret weapon in disguise! Well, exposed for the moment.

Fortunately by that point, she'd pulled up the black skirt

which flared though it was short, too. Pink vines swirled up the side, managing to go rather nicely with her underwear though only she and I knew that now. The pink blouse she stuck her arms into finished off the ensemble in style as she began to button the oversized black buttons closing them over a lacy pink bra she filled out more than adequately. She left the side zipper of the skirt apart a moment while tucking in the bottom of the blouse. "There!" she said, arms outward like a performing artist. "Presto-chango. Better?"

"Barely!" I laughed, repeating her own word meaning much more now.

She refastened the seatbelt even though we were now creeping towards the entrance for an empty parking space. "Sorry about the striptease, Nicky. But I know how important first impressions are if we hope to get something out of these people."

After the rawness of all that coughing, my throat couldn't quite respond.

"What's the matter?" she said slyly as she brushed at the front of her skirt. "Cat got your tongue?"

I ahemmed again. It was becoming a signature caesura.

She looked around at the cup holders in the console and didn't see anything. "You need a drink?"

I bobbled my head like a dashboard figurine. Much easier than trying to answer intelligently.

Then quickly she withdrew a small plastic bottle from her purse. "Voila!" she beamed. "I come equipped with everything you could want!"

Good thing in my present state I couldn't respond to that

line either.

I took a much-needed swig—and coughed even more. I did finally swallow some down the right pipe. Then I regarded her longer than I should have. She still somehow looked like a young girl—but one that now oozed assured sexuality. The shortness of the skirt certainly helped. I jerked us finally to a stop at a parking stall marked "Visitor" quite close to the entrance.

She braced her arms against the dashboard. "Wow," she said. "It doesn't take much to turn your head, does it."

I finally managed to get enough saliva back in my mouth to answer, trying to come across as suave. "You underestimate your powers, my dear."

"I thought this would act as a power suit," she said. "I want you to be proud of me."

I tried to compose myself, a difficult enough task because I kept looking down at her shapely, bare legs much more exposed than before in the other outfit. "Let's just say you have a leg up on the competition."

That elicited another giggle. Did I have her in my pocket—or was I now in hers—even though she had none showing?

When we got out, she wreathed her arm in mine. A sound follow-up.

We climbed the extensive semi-circular steps to the towering glass atrium entry where we passed through a security scanner archway towards a crescent-shaped reception center flanked by two security guards and manned by a svelte young lady with emerald eyes, bobbed black hair and a similarly crescent smile. She greeted us cheerily, asking whether we had an appointment. Her simple nameplate in front of an angled control panel with its flickering buttons read, "Ashley Britton."

I announced myself as "Detective Christmas" and "my partner Ms. Degrotti," lending her more credibility, I hoped, since she was clearly close in age to the receptionist. Randi acknowledged the gesture with a confident nod and a side glance my way that, I swear, made her crystal blue eyes twinkle. "It's vital, Miss Britton, that we talk with Mikel Arkov and Sasha Borishnikol who may be able to shed some light on a crime against our clients." I displayed my license with élan.

She breathed in slowly. I think my addressing her more formally had given her pause, guessing most visitors likely used her first name. "I'm afraid Doctors Arkov and Borishnikol are too busy this morning to see anyone."

I tried a firmer tack. "It would behoove either of them to see us now, rather than the authorities later. We need to know where they were on the night a week ago when the crime occurred."

Randi moved forward then. "If they can convince us of their whereabouts then, we'll make sure no one else disturbs them again."

That seemed to fluster her even as it motivated. "I'll see what I can do." She rang them using her headset. "I left a message for either of them to contact the desk if they return soon to the office they share—and that it was in their best interests. Is that good enough?"

"It'll do," I said.

"You can wait a while in the lobby there." She gestured at the mauve and gray furnishings laid out in a circle around a central column that mirrored the curve of the information desk like an architectural ripple. No one else occupied the space. The place didn't feel like one that welcomed visitors much.

While we waited there feeling rather conspicuous, Randi crossed a leg over the other, jiggling it, winning the attention of the two male guards who pretended they hadn't noticed. She smiled at them, giving a small girly wave. Both actually reddened, looking deliberately away.

"Practicing for later?" I whispered.

"I might as well since we may not have the chance."

But a few minutes later, Ashley beckoned us over to the half-window with a come-on scoop of a hand that flashed long black fingernails. "Dr. Arkov has a few moments while he's checking his messages."

"That's all we'll need," I replied.

"Just follow the prompts on the elevator's screen to his office on the second floor," Ms. Britton intoned. "I'll log you in. But please go only there and come right back. Access elsewhere requires security badges."

I nodded as she took our business cards, Randi casting a sly glance back at the guards with a smile before we headed for the elevators. The screen beside the up and down buttons flashed blue, announcing which letter elevator would be available before flashing the floor it was destined for.

"Very state of the art," I said.

"Technological frou-frou," she sang back. "People are still just people."

"Feeling our oats, are we?"

"Trying to," she grinned.

We followed the arrowed signs in the hallway to "Arkov/Barishnokol # 233" and knocked on the door. It slid aside like something out of "Star Trek." A man close to my age in a long white lab coat looked up briefly, raising a finger because he was just ending a call on a video screen before pointing to the two chairs at the side of a small acrylic desk. We didn't sit, though, knowing we'd maintain an upper hand more by standing, especially Randi. The screen retracted back into the desktop, still visible from its well. He fingered a shock of black hair away from crinkled gray-blue eyes, then shifted his stare from Randi's legs to me uncertainly, his wedge-shaped chin jutting out. Well, her outfit had caught his eye, however briefly. At least he was human.

I introduced us formally, presenting only our cards. Grudgingly, he shook both our hands with a rigid grip that made Randi wince more, I think, because his were strikingly cold. Then his tired eyes traced Randi more from top to bottom—or rather bottom to top—widening as if he'd just awakened from a grim trance.

"Am sorry," he said in a voice like Cary Grant's but with an accent that clicked out the consonants like a cricket. "We must have cold for test." He reached for a paper cup of coffee and held it with both hands, turning sideways to glance down through the bank of glass that overlooked a lab below, blinds open wide. We could see technicians in white smocks scurrying back and forth among flashing lights from gadgets resembling the futuristic toys Q might show off to James Bond. Some machines emitted cauliflower-shaped plumes of orange smoke. We couldn't hear a thing, though, the window clearly sound-proofed. When he turned back towards us again, we both realized his face was so ruddy it looked burned. "What detective want with us? We have much work."

"We understand you know Wade and Adeline Huntington," I started.

He looked up at the ceiling a moment as he sipped from the cup which he still held with both hands. "I think we meet at event last month." He left out the "h" in "think." "Why you ask?"

Randi picked up the ball then. "You were invited to a dinner with them a week ago but never showed or told them why you didn't. We'd like to know why."

"What day you mean? I not remember this." He fixed us with a beady stare.

I identified the date as last Saturday before Randi added, "Something went missing that night," she went on. "Something you apparently hoped to see?"

His high forehead wrinkled. "We look to crystals for the power. You mean this, yes?"

I thought of something else that might spark his memory. "You know their daughter, Mena Vandemere?"

He lifted his chiseled chin but shook his head no.

Randi looked across at me with a crooked smile.

Arkov stood stiffly upright. Undue hubris—or was he

anxious for us to leave? Maybe both.

Randi and I repressed our grins as she nudged me unobtrusively. I knew what she was hinting at. If this was it, we had to go for the coup de grâce. I drew out the copy of the check from the inside pocket of my jacket—the side without the empty holster—and displayed it like a banner on his desktop. "You don't know anything about this check from your company then?"

He actually backed up at my flourishing the paper, dismissively sweeping his large hand. "We are physicists. Not deal with such things." He pointed imperiously at the hall. "You need Finance."

Randi made a show of pulling me back by the crook of my arm, affecting the pretense, I think, of appearing to side with the doctor. But he'd already started for the door, pushing us back there. "I must rejoin Sasha."

I thanked him more than he deserved, unable to hold back a trenchant tone.

With raised chin again, he repeated, his record stuck, "We are scientists."

But before he could open the door, a hand lightly touching the small of Randi's back, the door swung open, startling even our reluctant interviewee.

"Mikel, why you not answer? We need you back—"

A tall woman with a long, full face featuring eyes so dark they looked black against the stark white of her short open lab coat, gawked at us, surprised at first, then acting offended as her fist tightened over something in her left hand. "You *reporters?*" She spat out the last word like an expletive.

"Detective, Sasha," declared Dr. Arkov with clenched jaw, scowling at me in particular.

"Dr. Barishnikol, I presume?" said Randi, reaching out and pumping her right hand so enthusiastically she nearly bowled the poor girl over. "It's a privilege to meet you!" I started to drag her toward the hall, seeing that we'd hit a brick wall here.

Sasha appraised Randi up and down with more of a frown before glowering at Mikel and the opened blinds of the long, wide window that spanned the other side of the office. "You let them see—lab?"

I followed up Randi's effusiveness with a quick shake of her free hand, too, and a salutary flair. "Pleased to meet you, too, Doctor."

She broke the touch and shuffled across to Mikel as if we'd contaminated her. "You call security?"

"Mr. Christmas—he is done here," he returned looking to us for confirmation.

"Thank you both for your time," I said with a bow from my neck and closed the door behind us, hastening for the elevators casting a backward glance over my shoulder to make sure they hadn't sicced Russian wolfhounds on us.

Randi whispered sharply, "Well, *that* went well."

"Did you see anything down there in the lab," I muttered, "we weren't supposed to?"

"Looked like kids running amok in a toy store," she shrugged.

"We did learn something, though," I said, scrambling for something positive.

"And what might that be, Nicky? Ruffling feathers can be fun?"

"They know more than they're letting on."

"Big whoop. Didn't we figure that going in?"

We strode back to the entrance leaving Ashley and the guards in our dust, the guards tensing defensively as if they half-expected to be called into action. All show, though, and no go—what security guards are often good for.

Only when we made it outside in the warming morning did I realize it. "He kept the copy of the check."

"It's just a copy. What does it matter?"

"But why would he?"

At first I was going to pass it off as an act by an absent-minded professor until it dawned on us both.

Randi voiced it first. "He wanted to know more about it, too."

I smiled, putting fingers to my temple at her impromptu divining. "Anything else, Madam Zola?"

"I think I got this one," she smiled back. "The two of them have more than just a working relationship?"

I bowed to her more melodramatically. "He kept using 'we.'"

"It could have been the royal 'we,'" she said. "They did act pretty snooty."

"They might be simply a link in a chain that we've at least rattled."

We both looked around as we left the complex, still expecting someone to follow. But nothing happened that we could see then. Paranoia fanned by our feeling like gadflies?

Then again that was part of our job, too.

As we headed now for the other couple to downtown Portland's new University of Oregon satellite annex under the White Stag "Portland, Oregon" sign, Randi turned towards me, elbow on the lowered arm of her captain's chair. "Did you catch what 'Natasha' was carrying in her hot little hands?"

"They really were hot, weren't they?" I agreed, wondering about the discrepancy between hers and Mikel's and what that implied about whatever project they'd come from.

"It made her left hand even redder when she clenched it closed."

"What did you see?" She was holding off, keeping me in suspense, her "everybody loves a mystery" surfacing again that made me so crazy with curiosity.

"I'd swear, Nicky," she said with a perplexed stare, "it looked like a *ruby!*"

10

When I could see the building through the windshield, I said, "What do we already know about the Kaslowskis before we meet them in person? You're becoming something of my 'Paula' Drake here."

"Your *what*?"

I kept forgetting how young she was. "You know, *Paul* Drake. Perry Mason's factotum?"

"'Factotum,' Nicky?" she mocked but with oblique admiration that I ate up more. There was still hope for her generation yet.

"You know, his 'go-fer.'"

"So why not just say 'go-fer' like a normal PI?"

"It doesn't have quite the cachet as 'factotum.'"

"'Cachet'? Enough already, Nicky!"

"I'm trying to lend a little class to our banter."

"Sometimes," she said, screwing her mouth to one side

in an even cuter smirk, "it's 'classier' just to chat with a regular guy."

"You want me to be *normal*?"

She just shook her head. "I don't know about you, Nicky. Sometimes you're a mystery all your own—fascinating but frustrating."

"The kind that everybody loves?"

"Getting there!" she laughed heartily from deep down in her throat, the type I found so endearing. "All I've learned so far from the internet is that the couple got married when they were both in graduate school at Washington State and are respected in their field of archeology, having published some of their findings."

"Anything that might tell us why they'd be interested in this diamond?"

"Well, they do seem to specialize in the 'woo-woo factor.'"

Now she was putting me on the defensive. "The *what*?"

"You know, fanatical religious mumbo jumbo ancient peoples believed in that involved rare stone carvings thought to be talismans or amulets."

"Ancients did think the shinier stones captured power from the skies because they looked like the stars," I said, "Essentially it's called 'sympathetic magic.'"

She stared at me, surprised. "Where'd *that* come from?"

"Folklore fascinated me when I was growing up, maybe because my mom was so superstitious."

"And you thought *I* was full of surprises."

"Does that mean we're more evenly matched now?" I

smiled.

She ruffled her skirt back and forth, unintentionally showing me more leg. "You tell me!"

"No fair!"

We ended up at a parking structure nearby, giving up on finding a place on the street that dead-ended because of the freeway and the Willamette River below. I hadn't been able to reach the Kaslowskis when I'd called the numbers posted in the university directory online while Randi was scanning her laptop.

"Didn't spring term just end?" she said when I mentioned that. "They might be busy getting in their grades."

"Always giving people the benefit of the doubt."

"Guilty until proven innocent," she smiled back.

When we entered the brick building's ground floor, we saw the "receptionist" this time was a very young man paging through a comic book or "graphic novel" as they're called now, not exactly promising intellectual fodder for someone representing a university. He did look up when we approached—but only to regard Randi who gave him the one-two punch by batting her blush-colored eyelids at him and whisking that skirt back and forth again. I feared, though, this might be more a classic case of casting pearls before swine.

When he answered my question about seeing either of the Kaslowskis, I began to despair that my initial assessment had been uncomfortably accurate.

He grinned moronically at Randi. "They're not here." What little brain power he might have had before, however negligible, had by now definitely done an Elvis and left the building.

"Why couldn't you tell us that over the phone when we called?" I grumbled.

"It's summer break for most of us." He finally turned toward me with vacant eyes peering out of a can-shaped head made worse by his Tom Hanks crewcut. "I'm filling in here on work study to make some extra bucks for fall term."

"And Ah don't know nothin' 'bout birthin' babies," I half -expected him to add though I'd already come to that conclusion. My faith in the younger generation foundered again. Thank heaven for the likes of Randi!

"Well, is there anyone here who *does* know how we might get hold of the Kaslowskis?" said Randi coming to the rescue even though she'd already felled another hapless victim who, frankly, didn't have far to go. While he seemed easy prey with those freckles across the bridge of his Archie nose, she did display preternatural powers that easily challenged any diamond's legendary ones.

The Alfred E. Neuman grin came on again. "There's just a skeleton crew here this time of year," he said, fumbling with the phone console. "But I've got just the one for you who's more in the know."

"Thank you," said Randi peering at his left breast where the name tag read, "Russell."

"Oh, call me, Russ," he said, blushing in streaks from the neck up as if suddenly on fire.

She repeated his nickname as though toying like a lioness with a certain kill.

A few moments later, an elderly woman clomped out of the glass door from the nearby office in a drab gray dress that I half expected to sport a huge sharp Maleficent collar in back, who scowled at "Russell." "I'm Mrs. Bailey," she said with a hand fiddling the black lanyard holding a pair of glasses at her sagging chest. "I understand you're looking for a couple of our faculty members?"

Then with some hesitation as her eyes darted from me to Randi and back to Randi again with an uncertain grimness that wrinkled her whole face, apparently weighing whether Randi was a student under the sway of some Svengali or if I might be the fatherly figure in her life. I had to help her lean towards the better take, blinking eyelids quickly, too, though it didn't work the same magic as when Randi had leveled it at the males we'd met. In fact, the gesture may have only deepened the creases in the woman's forehead. In a last-ditch effort for respect, I finally whipped out my license.

Fortunately, that made her shift her horned glasses more tightly against her eyes before pulling back some as though in horror.

"We're investigating the theft of a valuable artifact," I said, "that requires a consultation with the Kaslowskis for their expertise."

Randi lifted her sparkling eyes up at me with obvious respect again before turning towards Mrs. Bailey, showing that we made a pretty good team by grabbing onto my arm as well. That clinched it.

"Of course," said the matronly warden, softening somewhat into the registrar she really was. "They've just returned from their week-long dig south of Fossil and are staying the night here in Portland before their next fieldwork project. I understand that was the 'final' for their graduate seminar."

Randi and I shared a glance. They obviously had an iron-clad alibi for why they hadn't shown up for the dinner. But we still needed to know what their interest in the diamond might be.

"Could we find out where they're staying?" I said.

Again she hesitated. "This is important enough to disturb them now? They must be exhausted if they're taking time off up here. And they still have yet to turn in their grades for that class."

"It won't take us long to pick their brains," Randi added, seeing that implicit flattery for the faculty Mrs. Bailey represented had already worked wonders.

She raised her head at Randi, still with mixed feelings. I figured I'd better introduce her in a way that would erase any doubts, calling her my "assistant Miss Miranda Degrotti." That at least made her lower her head back down to normal eye level from staring up at the ceiling for rats that might be there somewhere.

Despite the extensive interior remodeling, this was still, after all, an old shell. I couldn't help thinking of it as an oversized version of Matryoshka dolls with a shiny new one nested inside. That incongruously expensive two-story maple staircase that climbed brightly up opposite Russell's receptionist desk against the ailing century-old brick wall stood out as an untoward reminder of that.

She then told us the Kaslowskis were "lodging" at the

Portland Hilton Executive Tower and asked if she could notify them first to make sure they wouldn't be unduly surprised at our visit.

"Sure thing, Mrs. Bailey," crooned Randi, turning very lady-like despite "Russ" still ogling her out the side of his pie -sized eyes.

"And assure them we won't need much of their time," I added hastily to secure our catch.

A few minutes later after Mrs. Bailey excused herself to make the call from her office, she returned saying she couldn't reach them but that she left a message with the concierge that we'd be dropping by soon.

On our way back to the basement parking area where we'd found a spot, Randi said as I opened the door for her again, "So what role do you want me to play this time, Nicky? Miss Goody Two-Shoes—or Trampy Vamp?"

"What's wrong with just being you?"

"You like me the way I am?" She fluttered her eyes at me, even though she knew she had me in the palm of her hand from the time she changed before my still-recovering eyes.

"That outfit has brought out the best in you so far."

"It could have just been you, too, you know."

"The best costume," I said, "is the one that doesn't seem like one. Isn't that the secret of acting, acting like you're not acting?"

She giggled. "That's exactly what our drama coach said in college."

When we finally arrived at the hotel's check-in counter,

after engaging in more urban warfare politely known as traffic congestion, it was later than I'd planned—nudging up against four o'clock. We asked the concierge whether the Kaslowskis had gotten our message.

The young lady whose name tag read "Molly" in a smart black uniform with white trim primped the back of her short black hair. She spoke in a surprisingly low soft voice for such a position. "When they checked in a little after one, they mentioned something about coming down to the lounge for a drink after they rested up."

"You let them check in that early?"

Molly glanced over at Randi who acknowledged her happy face by reflecting it. Remarkable that she could look so animated after a day that had so far tried our patience. "They're Hilton Honors members, so we found them a clean room before our normal check-in time, which would have been right about now. We do that whenever we can for our special guests." I think that was a little promotional plug thrown out there as a sop to Cerberus that Randi and I lapped up since she obviously considered us prospective candidates. Neither of us corrected her, though Randi smiled a bit self-consciously. We didn't want to lose her good graces.

I nodded back. "That's where we'll wait for them then."

"You're welcome to register for a room now, too, since we're not very busy," the girl said brightly. She must have just come onto her shift herself because she looked so fresh. Or maybe this was youth springing eternal to remind me of the one I'd lost—but had regained vicariously in my partner.

Randi giggled again at the suggestion, gesturing back and

forth with her fingers. "We're not—you know—like that."

"Oh," she said. "I'm sorry. I thought—"

"That's okay," said Randi, leaning affectionately against me, making things worse—or better. She was getting too good at mixed messages. "You're not the first to mistake us for an item."

"I didn't mean to offend," she apologized.

"It's more flattering than you realize," I said. I saw that Randi ate that up, too.

As we walked away towards the lounge after that fairly tame and understandable contretemps, Randi whispered to me, "Don't look so eager for happy hour while we've still got a job to do."

"Aren't you the one who told me we should make work seem fun?"

"What drove you to it this time?" she smirked. "The traffic?"

"Just the trigger," I said. "We're only trying to cater to the comfort of our subjects."

"'Subjects' rather than 'suspects'?"

"Yet to be determined."

"I guess the more relaxed everyone is," she sighed, "the more honest they'll be. You're getting pretty good at luring me into the act yourself."

I again pretended to brush knuckles at my lapel. "All the best directors do."

She batted at my arm again as we entered the open lounge now called—a bit crassly, I thought for a Hilton—the Hop City Tavern. I regretted not being able to show Randi the 32nd floor lounge and fine dining restaurant with its breathtaking cityscape executives had seen fit in their dubious wisdom to convert to more lucrative convention rooms. We located a table near the entrance in sight of the registration counter that seemed appropriate for our fact-finding-mission in an interview we hoped wouldn't seem like one, the best kind. "Is it possible? You're finally winding down?"

"You make me sound like a wind-up doll, Nicky," she said, her eyes catching the flickering of the candle on the table, almost calling into question that claim.

"Much more than that," I smiled though she was half-right.

"But the prospect of a drink and hors d'oeuvres do make me a little weak in the knees. Not to harp on it, but we did miss lunch again, you know."

"Sorry about that," I said. "Will this make up for my sin of omission?"

She gave me a crooked smile. "You do seem to be making up a lot lately, don't you think?"

"Don't they say that making up is the best part?"

"It's not *that* kind of making up—is it?"

I skirted that issue for now, not realizing how that sounded. "Martinis don't offer much nutritional value."

She sat down, yanking her skirt down in preparation for this next coming-out party. "Drinks stimulate the appetite, Nicky—as if I needed any more stimulation."

I was thinking the same thing. "I'll make sure to order us both two olives apiece then. How's that?"

"Not much nutritional value in olives," she retorted.

"Maybe I'll order something that will win them over into opening up more—and sate my partner's appetite."

"Is that what you think drinks and appetizers will do for me?"

"You'll be my test case," I smirked.

"This is a *test*?" she laughed.

"It should be a breeze for you," I grinned, "since you've already passed the others with flying colors."

Then I heard her stomach make gurgling noises. "Oh, darn! I'm giving myself away!"

"In your own winning way," I chuckled.

But out the side of my eyes from where we sat, I noticed a strange, young hippie-looking couple in drab clothing loitering in the lobby, the man in a stained-band floppy hat and what looked like a serape, the girl in a sloppy hoodie watching me with dark, slanted eyes. They didn't seem the type to be waiting around to register.

"What is it, Nicky?" said Randi. "You seem jumpy."

I nodded. "Maybe a little. I'm not sure we're on the right track with these people." I didn't want to call her attention to something that might be nothing and upset her when she was finally settling down.

Randi shifted around following my eyes but the couple had disappeared. "Maybe you *do* need a drink." She flagged down the barmaid at the far end of the bar wearing a black tunic for a dress with white piping set off by dark netted stockings that did seem like a classier if somewhat dated touch, alerting her that we expected another couple shortly. She placed four cocktail napkins imprinted with the Romanesque "H" on the round table. I asked her name since I couldn't quite make it out on the nameplate across her small chest and didn't want to embarrass myself by staring, eyes falling to her netted legs that Randi caught with the beginning of a frown.

"Shirley," said the barmaid in her high-pitched voice that reminded me of the actress Glenne Headly.

I then ordered Beefeater dry martinis "up" accompanied by "soda backs" with lots of ice since I convinced Randi they went down better with a chaser despite the way James Bond ordered them. I also knew carbonation could quicken the liquor to the blood stream aside from making the drink more palatable. I needed the effect to steel me for the meeting, for one thing, but also finding it easier to gauge when I'd had enough. At Randi's insistence, Shirley brought the drinks with *three* olives apiece instead of just two, seeming unusually thrilled at this request. A slow day, I guess. "Enjoy, you two lovebirds!" Then she flitted back to this end of the bar. I could have sworn I'd seen shadows at the far end where I'd noticed her straightening the seams of her stockings earlier.

"We don't want *too* much of an empty stomach, do we," she whispered afterwards, "or you'll have to pick me up off the floor."

"Not exactly the impression I'm shooting for in front of these distinguished professors."

Randi quickly demolished the olives just as a couple came up to us tentatively that made us both start. I guess the sips of martinis followed by gulps of the sodas didn't hasten the liquor's effect quite *that* fast.

"Are you the ones looking to consult with us?" said the tall man in a black blazer adorned with the image of a golden lion on a red badge sewn onto his right breast pocket. He adjusted the skewed blue buttoned-down shirt collar, head bent with a strange intensity heightened by agate-brown eyes on a deeply tanned face contributing to a rugged handsomeness.

"Dr. Kaslowski?" I ventured reaching up with my hand as I half-rose.

"And," smiled Randi, getting up, too, but extending her hand towards the woman beside him with an equally sun-tanned, but much smoother complexion accentuated by a short black evening gown, long brunette hair fanning over one bare shoulder, "the other Dr. Kaslowski?"

They both chuckled awkwardly. "I guess," she said in a husky Debra-Winger voice, "we'd better chuck the titles, hadn't we?"

They introduced themselves then as Kane and Ava while we reciprocated with our first names, too, though I used Randi's more formal "Miranda" since it seemed more fitting here.

"You certainly don't look like archeologists," I said.

"As much as you do detectives," Kane rejoined as he regarded Randi's outfit, then his wife's, presumably comparing the length of their skirts. Randi's trumped hers by at least two inches making her tug it down where it wasn't going to go any further as both women wriggled to hide that part of their wardrobe.

I laughed back. "I'm actually a private eye, Miranda here, my confidential secretary cum partner, if you will." Randi beamed at that intro as I encouraged them to order whatever they'd like because it was on us, since we hoped they might tell us more about our client's artifact.

"Ah," said Kane, his interest obviously piqued. "I see."

Ava gazed longingly at our martinis so that Randi beckoned Shirley back circling her hand at their drinks with her eyebrows raised. "We're having Beefeater martinis with soda backs." I think she was showing off her newfound drink jargon so they didn't think her too young.

Ava sighed. "Let's splurge, honey. We've earned it."

Kane nodded with an indulgent smile and Shirley endorsed the selection with a hearty, "Super choice!" She swept ringlets of black hair away from her ears sporting simple but stunning diamond studs before swinging back to the bar where she now had a TV silently broadcasting CNN. She carried the drinks over on a tray, crowding the small table with the glasses of soda so that it was hard to tell whose was whose.

"Another round for you two, too?" she asked us, giggling at the "tu-tus."

"When you can," I said.

"I'm all yours except for that other couple over there," she noted. Then she noticed I'd dropped some of the tiny ice cubes into my martini. "And maybe a glass of just ice?"

"How thoughtful." I'd noticed that Randi had winced a little at the first taste. She could use some, too, not used to a drink this strong.

"Surely," she bleated back with a canny smile. Could someone so young know the wordplay on her name from the 1980 movie "Airplane"? Or was she just naturally so self -effacing? I guess we could fill in the blanks any way we wanted. I preferred to think she was clever. I was pretty sure from Randi's face she thought the girl was flirting with me and bucking for a good tip, probably more the case than my more generous slant.

Shirley delivered the glass of ice and even a spoon which restaurants seemed reluctant to provide nowadays without considerable prompting. Who would want to pilfer a spoon? We hadn't even looked at the bar menu but I asked whether she had something like spinach dip with flatbread or taco chips.

"A house specialty!" she beamed. "And I can bring it with both if you want."

"Very accommodating, isn't she?" said Randi with an eyebrow highly arched.

Ava bent down to sip at the overfull martini glass so as not to spill it but holding back her brunette strands still a little damp, I thought, from having apparently taken a shower in their room and not drying it enough.

"Now," said Kane getting down to business, "how can we help?"

So I did the same. "We understand you knew something about the diamond owned by Wade and Adeline Huntington."

"Ah," he said again. "Mr. Huntington sparked our interest in it at the Doernbecker charity ball at the Crystal Ballroom last month."

"Seems," I said, "he attracted a lot more attention there than he should have."

"He did seem unusually forthcoming with perfect strangers," Kane continued. "We knew about its historical importance, of course, but also some of the tales that grew up around a gem as notorious as that one."

Ava picked up on the story. "It's suspected to be one of the two jewels that made up the eyes of a statue depicting Lakshmi, the golden Indian goddess of wealth, said to give off magical powers at certain times of the year when the sun struck the diamonds just so."

Randi looked goggle-eyed at all this. "Nothing like the end of the world or anything as awful as what they're saying about the upcoming Super and Blood Moons, I hope."

"Not quite that dramatically eschatological," Ava said with a throaty chuckle. "One legend says that if the jewels are ever replaced back in the lost statue, the avatar may actually come back to life. That may just be colorful wishful thinking, of course."

"It's not unusual either," Kane added, "that precious jewels like diamonds ancients believed captured the power of the sun since some could actually fluoresce in darkness."

"'Sympathetic magic'!" Randi piped up, gulping at the glass of soda which she didn't realize was meant for Ava. So my girl had actually listened to me! I flushed with pride.

Kane's close-mouthed smile and blue eyes glittering in the candlelight made him look very much like Harrison Ford just then. I was afraid Randi might have thought so, too, by the way she glowed back at him herself. I felt that prickling at the back of my neck again. "Quite so, dear girl."

I followed up. "You mentioned some of these things to Wade?"

"He pooh-poohed the more outlandish tales," said Kane now, "until we explained some attributes could be tested with today's sophisticated instruments."

"We're really euhemerists at heart," Ava nodded. "There's often some historical truth to these myths. Only one case in point is Heinrich Schliemann's discovery in the 19th century that Troy really did exist beyond Homer's heroic tales—nine of them, in fact, one atop the other."

"Ancient cultures," Kane interjected, "often did show an uncanny ability to erect structures that take into consideration astronomical events, like finding that the 5,000-year-old Stonehenge may have been built to mark the beginning of the Druidic year as the time of the summer solstice, for instance."

"Which is," I said, "this Sunday, isn't it?"

They both nodded as Shirley delivered the hors d'oeuvres along with small plates, taking away the empty glasses and seeing that Randi's and my martinis were nearly empty. She raised her eyes at me and I nodded back. The two archeologists spooned the dip into their plates and both chose the flatbread over the chips while Randi and I preferred the crunch of the chips.

Randi stared at the two of them a moment, taken in by their enthusiasm and knowledge as I was, but hesitating before finally speaking up. "You haven't heard then what's happened."

"Heard what?" said Ava.

Randi gave me a knowing glance and gulped again at the soda just as Shirley delivered our second martinis. "Don't you think we should tell them, Nicky?"

She was putting our privileged confidence on the line but I could see why. They seemed sincerely in the dark. I clasped my hands together on the table. "I'm sorry to say," I said slowly, "the stone's been stolen."

Their eyes blinked widely. "A 99-carat diamond?" said Kane.

"At the anniversary dinner, in fact," Randi replied. "During the night after a blackout caused by the thunderstorm."

Ava sipped again at her martini. "While they were there?"

I opened out a hand in frustration. "As unlikely as that sounds."

Kane took a bite of the triangular flatbread with its tip full of the dip. "What a terrible loss! We were so involved with getting the kids to set up camp at the dig the past week that we completely forgot about that dinner invitation."

"A great experience for that class, though," Ava added. "Two students stood out enough that we hired them as assistants this summer. Sam Dekker and Elaine Schatz have a bright future ahead of them as a team. It helps that I think they're sweet on each other."

"You probably don't know then that the Huntingtons are planning to renew their marriage vows this Sunday," I said since they had the best alibi in the book.

They shared a glance, but Kane was the one who answered. "How could we? But we've got fieldwork on the docket with our assistants that day anyway, assuming everything pans out."

"It's Father's Day to boot," I conceded. "To be honest, their party may not have as many people attending as they think."

But that's when I first noticed Randi had grown paler. She was drinking martinis, though, on an empty stomach. Usually mere fatigue gave her cheeks a flushed patina that made her look even prettier. Not now.

Randi wiped a finger at her forehead uncertainly. "I don't understand this trend toward renewing marriage vows. Isn't a vow a vow?" She wasn't slurring her words but her lips pinched together at the side as if she were experiencing pain but didn't want to show it.

Ava offered a winsome smile, placing her hand atop her husband's. "You might understand down the road." She hesitated, thin eyebrows wrinkling. "Are you okay, honey?"

Randi looked at me instead, head tilting, a hand webbed across her stomach. "Nicky? I don't feel so very good."

Ava leaned towards her. "Maybe we should both go to the little girl's room?"

Randi scooted her chair back, trying to get up but staggering so that I had to reach out to hold her arm. Her voice small, she answered, "Okay."

"This is all my fault," I said. "All she's had to eat with me today are those olives."

Ava put a hand to her mouth. "Oh, no." She glanced at her husband.

Shirley looked up from her television set and started to come over. "You mind, Kane, if I go with them? I feel responsible." I held onto Randi's other side.

"I'll hold down the fort," he assured me, Shirley asking if we needed anything.

"Maybe some more soda?" I said, seeing that it might be remedial later.

She nodded and we three made our way to the rest room. "Could you make sure no one else is in there?" I said to Ava at the door. "I'd like to help her inside."

She eyed me skeptically. "She must be some private secretary."

"I'm—more than that," Randi managed weakly.

"Believe me," I said, "we've had some experience sharing each other's rest rooms." Most decidedly at the end of the last case when we uncovered the truth about the hostage and his keepers, something we could never explain.

"Do tell," Ava remarked as she eased open the door, checked around, then beckoned us both in, resuming her hold on Randi's other side while we all entered.

"I'd better take it from here," I said. "Could you stand guard?"

Reluctantly Ava stayed inside at the door, forehead creased, uncertain what I was really doing there.

"I've really got to—" Randi said, retching already but not yet bringing anything up.

"I know, honey," I cooed, trying to calm her self-consciousness about the inevitable. "Erpsville."

I rushed her to the sink but on a whim and a sneaking suspicion since this wasn't at all like her, I insisted she use the stopper. "Oh, no, Nicky! I don't want you to see—"

"Go ahead, sweetie." I pulled her hair to the back of her neck in a makeshift ponytail so she wouldn't get any on the strands as she bent over. "It's okay."

Then she threw up so easily it seemed like she'd just turned on a faucet. I certainly wasn't like that when I did the deed. That's why I always resisted the urge, often to my detriment especially when I was younger. For me it felt as if I were turning myself inside out, roaring like a grizzly caught in a bear trap. Not so her. My God, she even vomited daintily!

"Nicky?" she said, faintly wobbling a little, so I had to hold her by her shoulders as she lifted her head back up. "You'd better look after all."

I stared down at the sink. Flecks of green olive floated in a small pool of watery bile with a trickle of red swirling like tiny snakes amid the ice she'd brought up. Then because of the body heat from having been in her stomach, we realized the two or three pieces hovering over the metal stopper weren't ice.

Randi's voice crackled. "Diamonds?"

I beckoned Ava to come over. "Oh, my poor dear," she said to Randi, a hand on her shoulder, too.

"Hardly." I reached down gingerly with thumb and forefinger and placed the three pieces on paper toweling. "It's *chips of glass!*"

"Oh, my God," Ava gasped.

"But it's not from her glass of soda," I pointed out as I gaped at Ava. "It's from the one meant for *you!*"

Ava backed up. "What the hell's going on here anyway?"

11

When we brought out the chips in the paper toweling to show the barmaid, she was equally horrified.

"You didn't fill the glasses yourself?" I said.

Shirley shook her head vehemently, pointing. "I welcomed another couple over there before I brought your second round from the bar," she insisted. "Someone must have dropped something in that drink when my back was turned."

I thought of that shabbily dressed pair I'd seen lingering near the hotel lobby.

The assistant hotel manager joined us at that point, a middle-aged woman in a tailored dark blue pants suit with flared bellbottoms named Miriam Williams. "The bartender isn't scheduled to show up until five—and he's late," she told us. "Nothing like this has ever happened here on my watch." She apologized effusively, offering to treat all of us to a free meal and even assuring the Kaslowskis they would not be charged for the night they were staying there. "We'd like to offer you a complimentary night as well," Ms. Williams said, eyeing Randi in particular.

"Oh, thank you," Randi blushed regaining too much color though it was welcome whatever the reason. "But we're—just—partners?" It didn't quite explain our situation but the lady got the idea.

"You swallowed bits of glass, my dear," she persisted. "We have to compensate you somehow. How about a rain check you can use anytime you like?"

"I can't believe that's what happened," Randi said, a hand on her stomach, "and I lived through it!" She turned to me. "How is that even possible?"

"You're a very lucky young lady," said Ms. Williams. "The offer for a free dinner tonight still stands—*and* this voucher for two hundred dollars for you to use any way you like."

She must have feared a law suit though that wasn't our style. But we couldn't fault her solicitude.

"We actually have somewhere to go before our day's officially over." I wasn't eager to eat here because of the café's very limited fare anyway. But why would we after an experience like this that demonstrated at the very least some degree of negligence?

She fluttered the vouchers like a flag of truce—which they were, of course—so that Randi gamely accepted them as we turned around.

"And if you have any doctor bills, believe me," Ms. Williams added, "we'll cover them."

"She must have some constitution," I said. "I don't think that'll happen."

"The bar bill is on the house, too, right, Ms. Williams?" Shirley offered as well.

"Absolutely." She regarded the Kaslowskis now, knowing they were officially their guests anyway, who looked cowed by the whole experience.

Randi fixed my eyes uncertainly. "My stomach's really empty now—but I don't think I'm ready to eat anything just yet either."

"It'll take a while to recuperate," I said.

Kane and Ava both indicated the appetizer. "Why don't you take some of this home with you?" Kane said. "We feel guilty hogging it."

"Thanks," I said. "We've had plenty. Enjoy it for yourselves."

Kane whispered as if someone might be listening in since Ava had clearly explained the mix-up of the glasses. "Why would anyone target my wife when we aren't even part of this game—whatever it is?"

"Good question," I said. It had certainly added a different dimension to this case.

They stood stone-still for a moment, a stance I took to mean they were honestly baffled. "Try to enjoy the rest of your time off," I said.

"Hard to do when someone might be after us for God knows what," said Ava.

"I think we'll feel safer getting back to fieldwork," Kane

tried to joke. "That has dangers of its own but ones at least we're used to."

"One more reason," I answered, "we hope to bring this case to a conclusion by this Sunday." Not to mention that bonus Mena had dangled before us.

"Good luck with that," said Kane with a half-smile that showed his support, as well as a healthy dose of doubt.

We exchanged business cards. "Tell us if anyone tries to bother you again. It might give us another lead to follow up on."

"Don't worry," said Ava. "We will." She reached for Randi without actually touching her. "You take care of this girl, will you?"

"Part of my job, too," I smiled back as we waved and took our leave for the parking garage.

"Interesting," Randi murmured in the humming stillness of the elevator, "that Ms. Williams thought we were together, too. We must be giving off pheromones or something!"

"'Pheromones'?" I chuckled. But that may not have been the malapropism it seemed.

"Well, an *aura* then!" she amended.

I used the van's fob to unlock the van so I could see the reassuring lights flash on, not remembering exactly where we'd parked it. This experience had addled me. The scare over Randi had been sobering in more ways than one, undercutting any pleasant effect we might have enjoyed from the martinis. I think the same was true for Randi. Her pallor had returned, making me hang onto her arm just in case. I helped her inside, got into the driver's seat and found our way into the thick of going-home traffic I'd hoped to avoid.

"We're still going to need some corroboration," I added, "to verify that our Russian friends were really working overtime on some special project."

"Maybe from those lab assistants we saw?"

"We need to make one more stop, you know, if you're up to it. We promised the Huntingtons we'd check in about the missus."

"Oh, Nicky," she groaned. "I'm going to need something to coat my stomach with soon—even if it's only Pepto Bismol. I mean, I swallowed *glass chips*, for crying out loud."

"We'll get you something, don't worry." I said. "But maybe the martinis did make it into your blood stream enough so you didn't feel them go down."

She played with the hem of her dress. "I'm sorry about fouling up the day like this."

"How could we know you'd be attacked by mistake? You're stronger than you think."

Her eyes flicked over at me. "Attacked," she said, mulling over the word. "Why would anyone try to hurt Ava of all people? You sure that wasn't really meant for me?"

Maybe I had mistaken the mix-up in the glasses. What if, in fact, the bits of glass had been meant for *me*? Our paranoia was having a field day.

When we stopped in front of the manor, the lights inside were already on though it wasn't yet twilight. That seemed odd. We knocked lightly rather than ringing the doorbell which would have set off old-fashioned Winchester chimes that took forever to finish tolling. We didn't want to wake Addy if she was sleeping. When Wade eased the door open, he looked gaunt and haggard.

"You remembered," he said with a lopsided smile.

"Is she any better?" said Randi even though we could already tell from his appearance.

He shook his head.

"You shouldn't take chances now," I said, wondering if it was food poisoning—or another kind.

"It's Thursday evening, Wade," said Randi, pushing the point for obvious reasons considering what had just happened to her. "ER won't be as crowded as it would on the weekend."

He looked at us after he ushered us inside. "You suppose someone could have slipped her a Mickey? Or do they even call it that anymore?"

"They have more modern versions since the days of Raymond Chandler," I said. But what if the robbers had tried to poison one of them or slip them sleeping pills, if they'd intended to steal the diamond one way or another the night of the dinner, not knowing about the fortuitous thunderstorm and power outage? Maybe the theft had actually been planned for when they fell asleep after dinner. "Some symptoms, though, would be the same."

He looked at us with a pathetic hang-dog expression. "You'd better see what you think."

Maria was bustling about the kitchen preparing some kind of chicken dish that we could smell already as we climbed the stairs, Randi hanging onto the banister more firmly, Wade trailing us with considerable effort.

When we entered the master bedroom at the end of the hall, it reeked of sickness, that indefinable mix of stuffiness, sweat and bile. Addy lay back on doubled-up pillows, white hair wildly streaming about her pallid face as if she were drowning, mouth open fish-like, eyes glassy and blinking repeatedly. It reminded me painfully of Angie towards the end. Randi and I both felt her forehead, though we could see the tell-tale flush of her face.

"She's burning up, Wade," Randi said. "What's her temperature anyway?"

"I couldn't keep the thermometer in her mouth," he said, voice watery.

"You don't have one of those new digital type that takes it through the ear or by holding it over her forehead?" I asked. I'd had that even for Angie.

"I know what you're thinking," he said, inconsolable. "A place that has everything doesn't have that?"

Maria appeared in the doorway, wiping the palm of one hand on her colorful apron. "Chicken broth again? She usually help."

Randi looked down again at Addy pressed deeply into the pillow. "Do you think you could swallow it?"

"Uh-uh," Addy rasped.

Randi tried to help her. "Can you sit up a little, Addy?"

She groaned, a hand flat on the bed as she pushed, Randi trying to lever her up but in vain, looking at her helplessly then over at me and Wade.

"We have to face the music, dearest," sighed Wade, approaching her but bent over like a question mark before turning about to tell Maria, "Better get Peter to bring her down."

"I call," said Maria who made her way back down to the intercom's central station in the kitchen. Moments later Peter tramped up the stairs, reaching down to pick her up, then faltering. "Shouldn't you be wearing something warmer, Miss Addy?" he said.

She barely moved her head.

"She's sopping wet in that nightgown," said Randi, barring him with an arm and nodding for us men to leave the room, shutting the door partway. In a few minutes, she said, "Okay. You can come back in."

With her now in a thick waffled pink robe, moaning lightly, Peter carried her effortlessly in his bulging arms.

"There, there," he said, surprisingly gentle. But as he passed me by, he whispered out the side of his wide mouth, "She feels like skin and bones." At the doorway he turned to make sure he could get her through without bumping her head against the jamb. "I'll get her to emergency at St. Vincent's in the Mercedes Sprinter," he said to Wade. "It's already outside the garage. Who's coming? I could fit all of you in."

Wade hesitated. "Me for sure—but I hate to leave the place—untended—with just you here, Maria. What if those thieves come back?"

"I keep dinner hot," said Maria from the door. "And I can use fry pan like bat." She gesticulated with one arm.

Randi smirked, patting at her thigh, looking at me, surprised. She'd forgotten we left our weapons in the glove compartment. "We could stay behind, Nicky, and do what we do best—protect and serve." She had the words down pat—but it seemed woefully out of place coming from her small frame just now after she'd already endured more than her fair share.

"Are you up to that?" I said. "It's been a rough day."

"Go be by your wife's side, Wade," Randi urged. "We'll stay until you call and tell us what's what."

His face relaxed as he tried a wan smile. "I know it's above and beyond the call of duty—but I'd be eternally grateful."

I gave him a pinched smirk. "We're a full-service agency."

"I make for you two then my chicken cacciatore," Maria brightened, obviously thrilled for the company. "With biscuit and gravy?"

"That's okay with you?" I said to Randi, knowing it wasn't quite the consolation dinner she might have chosen after her ordeal.

"Chicken should be easy on my stomach," she nodded.

I turned to Maria. "Frankly, you had me at the word 'biscuit.'"

"You're good people," said Wade with a half bow and shambled out behind Peter carrying Addy down to the front door as we followed. "I just hope I didn't wait too long."

"Call us the minute you know something?" said Randi with a half-wave at the entrance. He backhanded his acknowledgment. Then we watched them speed away in the

Sprinter, taillights blurring into the coming evening.

"Did she eat anything yesterday," I said to Maria as we accompanied her into the kitchen, "that anyone else didn't?"

She shook her head no. "Not since the lunch."

"It could just be a bug, I suppose," said Randi uncertainly. "Losing the diamond could have just lowered her resistance."

"We'll know soon enough," I said.

Maria served us the dinner in the corner dining room that admitted the setting sun framed by tied-back gauzy curtains. We asked her to sit with us but she politely declined, saying, "It is not proper."

Randi picked tentatively at the food with a fork at first, testing the hotness with a modest bite before swallowing, waiting a moment to see if her stomach could take it after what she'd been through. "Delicious," she finally said, giving out with a, "Hmmm," that brought a close-mouthed smile to Maria's broad face before she finished carrying in the side dishes.

We waited with coffee and her leftover dessert from the night before of angel food cake and fresh strawberries, but Wade didn't call until after eight.

"It's epiglottitis," he said, his dry voice cracking over the speaker phone. "She's in ICU, It'll be at least a couple of days for her to stabilize."

"I've never heard of that disease," Randi said on speakerphone.

"It's a very rare bacterial infection," he said, "but treatable with antibiotics they're feeding her with an IV." He hesitated as we read the silence as a tacit request.

"When will you be returning?" I said.

"They said I can stay overnight in the lounge until she improves enough for her to move to a regular hospital room."

Randi and I looked at each other, the quandary evident in our faces. "We—" Randi ventured, "—could maybe stay the night if you want."

"*Could* you?" said Wade. "We've got five bedrooms, you know. But isn't that asking too much?"

"We don't have a change of clothes," Randi objected in a whisper that I wasn't sure he heard. She did have what she'd left in the van, though, but I think she meant underthings.

I didn't want Wade to worry, though. We'd truly win him over with our sincerity here. He had enough to deal with right now anyway. But was it too much to ask of Randi? I looked to her but she gave a hesitant nod. "We can do that for tonight, I guess," I said before he hung up.

"This kind of illness came out of the blue," said Randi afterwards. "Not like what happened at the Hilton."

"We could be safer here," I offered.

"But how are we going to work this, Nicky?"

"We'll just have to make the best of it." I couldn't resist yawning, though. That caused Randi to do the same. "Can we alternate keeping watch every couple of hours?"

"After a day like this," she admitted, "it'll be hard."

But Maria took it all in stride more eagerly than we did. "You want for me to make up the beds in rooms upstairs?"

With some hesitation, Randi finally said, "We can bunk

right here if you give us some bedding. It'd be better for watching the grounds anyway."

"If we get too comfortable upstairs," I tried to joke, "we'd never wake up!" The deep brown cushions of the leather sofa and adjacent matching recliner covered with an afghan looked adequate—though I could see why Randi had been tempted with the mention of "beds."

"I get extra pillows," said Maria. "But you, Miss Randi. You sure you not want girl bedroom later?"

Randi paused again. "We don't have night things, Maria. Better to sleep in our clothes right here."

With a shrug, Maria left and brought down the bedclothes before taking her leave and retiring to her quarters.

"I can take first watch," I said.

"No, let me, Nicky—or I'll be the one who'll never wake up."

"You sure about that? I don't sleep very well anyway."

"Let's see how it goes. I'll go out and get our weapons."

"You can take the sofa," I said, pointing to the recliner for me where I then toed off my unlaced desert boots and settled in under the afghan as I angled the chair back. "Just tap me if you get too tired."

She went out and returned with my shoulder holster but sporting the Levi jacket I'd forgotten she'd left at the back of the van at the end of our last case. "It's a little nippy out there tonight so this feels good while I check around first."

"The alarm there," I said, indicating the console by the front door, "should cover the grounds right near the house if you remember to arm it when you come back in."

I looped the holster over the back of the nearby bentwood rocker but placed the Glock under the pillow. She then adjusted the waist of her skirt one way, then the other, the bottom of her garter holster showing slightly beneath that short hem.

"It's not likely they'd come back to the scene of the crime so soon, is it, Nicky?"

"Don't put anything past people," I cautioned sleepily. "Worst mistake a rookie can make."

"'Rookie,'" she mumbled. "I liked it better when you called me your 'Paula Drake.'"

That was the last thing I remembered until the hullabaloo made me bolt upright, heart jackhammering as I tumbled forward off the edge of the chair and staggered up from my knees to my stocking feet.

I clamped hands over my ears to mute the claxon of the alarm's 120 decibels. "What the hell?"

Randi was at the back patio door though I saw a butterflied copy of *People* on the floor next to one of the chairs where she'd been sitting earlier. That left it to me to disable the alarm groggily punching in the simple password Wade had given us, "Addy." Hand gripping her P-11, Randi slid open the sliding door with a nod for me to join her. I fumbled for the Glock, straining to step back into my boots, trying to ignore the hitch in my side from a hernia repaired some years back after I'd helped move a 350-pound big-screen Mitsubishi I should have saved for Superman.

Then together we scrambled to the backyard, where we tried to pursue two shadowy shapes flickering out of the glare of the floodlight into the distance that dipped towards that thread of Rock Creek at the end of the property. "What *happened*?" I managed.

She panted out, "They came up on the deck and rattled the glass trying to get in!"

The interlopers had sprinted far ahead of us already, better prepared for the slope than we were. I hadn't even tied my boots' shoelaces yet. The freshly cut lawn was also slick from being watered—and she was wearing only flats.

"Flashlight?" I said.

"Left it inside," she said.

All I had on me was Dad's lighter. So much for setting a good example.

Then we started slipping and sliding over each other like a modern-day Jack and Jill, much prettier in Randi's case since she was rolling over and over in that short skirt. We heard intruders splash across the creek followed by the twang of the wire mesh as they mounted the fence.

"Too late," I breathed. At least we'd seen that it was two people.

"I let you down, Nicky," she said, wiping at her smudged face.

"Could you see if they were armed?"

"I saw them in the floodlight."

We trudged back up the hill to the wood deck, she holding onto my arm pulling herself along as we crept back into the floodlight's cone. I looked down at her legs, this time for humanitarian reasons. Her calves and knees were streaked green and red from grass, dirt, and blood.

"Randi, you're hurt," I said.

She rubbed tentatively at one of the bruises around her broken skin. "I think I struck a sprinkler head or something." Then she pointed at my knees, my Levi's stained but the denim too hardy to have torn like her skin so thin I could make out her veins. "You didn't do much better."

"I had more protection."

"Some action heroes," she said.

I held onto her more tightly, lifting her somewhat from my side as we made our way to the sliding doors through which we could see a concerned Maria in her bathrobe now. Randi let me support her, telling me she was hurt more than she let on. "I've got to tend to your wounds."

"I think," she said slowly, "I should show you something first, Nicky. Can you get the flashlight Maria gave me that I left on the end table?"

"You have to do this now in the dark?"

"While they're still fresh," she said, looking up at the starlit night streaked with spectral cirrus clouds. "They might not be there tomorrow."

"But you're limping."

"I'm okay, really."

"Don't move. I'll be right back."

She held herself up with the help of the railing, looking off toward the eastern end of the house where the three-car garage lay.

I came back with the beam on. "Now what's so important that couldn't wait till morning?"

She tugged me towards the other end of the deck, round-ing the manor's corner, stopping at miniature rose bushes and a window that looked in at the dining room. She pointed and I aimed the beam down. I half-kneeled. "A footprint from what looks like a running shoe."

"No wonder they weren't slipping as much," she said. "I saw these *before* the alarm went off when I was casing the grounds before I checked the Hall of Fame to make sure everything was secure up there. They were here while we were eating dinner. But look closer."

I peered down more closely. "This one's small and narrow."

Randi nodded. "One of them is a *girl*."

12

"O Santo Cielos!" Maria slapped hands at her cheeks as we staggered in, bloodied but unbowed—well, sort of. "What you do, Senorita?"

"It's nothing really," Randi said. In a moment of quick thinking, Maria had grabbed a towel to lay down over the leather next to the end of the sofa where I'd tossed my afghan in a tangled ball. That was partly so her bare skin wouldn't stick—but also to blot the blood from her scratches.

"Is not nothing. Come with me and take off skirt. And oh my gosh. That blouse and nice jacket, too? I clean for you."

"Really?" said Randi. "It's a lot of bother."

"Now *my* job," she rejoined with a smile.

"I've had some medical training in the service," I said to put them both more at ease. "So you're in good hands."

Randi grabbed my smaller left hand. "You need some

cleaning up yourself." I'd fallen on both hands to catch myself, the knees of my Wrangler jeans taking the brunt of it.

"Grass stains only," I said. "No broken skin like you."

"Nice, soft hands, though," she added much to my dismay, and Maria's. Too soft, I thought. I was used to more callouses.

"Please come—and take off clothes?" said Maria. "I wash and give to you Miss Addy's robe."

Hesitating a moment, Randi then shrugged off the jacket that I noticed she'd kept on even after her initial forays outside, Maria hanging onto it with two fingers like holding a cat by the nap of its neck. Then Randi, wincing, hobbling to follow Maria into the utility room, returned wearing a chenille robe that she almost tripped over as its hem trailed over the carpet before she resumed her place on the towel.

"I should have worn jeans like you," Randi said.

"Wouldn't have worked as well as your outfit did with our scientists."

Maria plodded in with a metal box of medicine and bandages, which I opened before kneeling at her feet and gingerly parted her robe enough to examine the damage to her legs, while I carefully stretched her garter holster so I could slide it down her leg without touching her wounds.

I looked up at Maria. "We should wash off some of the grit first."

"I get for you." Then Maria brought a small plastic tub of hot water, a bath towel draped over her arm like a maitre d'. "I am nurse sometime here, too."

I dabbed the rag I squeezed into a ball to dab at the worst

abrasions, watching Randi's face to make sure I didn't hurt her too much. I looked over the sprays and tubes in the case for one that wouldn't sting, latching onto a can of Bactine.

"I'll have to clean up better than this later, you know."

"All in good time, my pretty," I said with apologies to the Wicked Witch. But at least it elicited a giggle from my favorite fan if not from Maria.

I sprayed the worst scratches first, blowing on them just to make sure they didn't hurt afterwards the way my mother had done, though I doubted that really helped. I was chary with the Bandaids, placing them only on the wounds that had bled the most. "You'll look like a patchwork doll when I'm done."

"A doll again," she clucked, then added, "Still, I've kind of got you where I want."

I looked up. "You mean me on my knees—your worship?"

She put a curled fist to her lips and giggled again. An easy audience.

I had to part the robe further up to reach the cuts on her thigh though Maria looked askance at me, making the sign of the cross. Of course I'd seen more before, though Maria didn't need to know that. "How did you get hurt so far up?"

"I wasn't wearing much to begin with, not like you while we rolled around on the grass."

I made a clicking sound out the side of my lips. "You do kind of throw yourself into your work."

"I didn't want them to get away. It was my responsibility."

"Ours," I corrected.

"I should have paid more attention, especially after I saw those footprints. I knew somebody had been out there—but thought they'd gone."

I leaned back on my haunches. "There. I think you're good."

"Not quite *yet*."

I regarded her eyes which twinkled a lighter blue somehow. "You're braver than you should be—but a good patient." I got back up.

"I take away now, yes?" said Maria of the kit, the wash bin and rag. I nodded as she looked to Randi now. "You need more, Miss Randi?"

"Maybe a couple of aspirins?" she answered. Maria smiled and left to get the bottle. She wriggled her toes on the carpet, fidgeting, wanting to get more comfortable but knowing she couldn't now. "You know, Nicky, those couldn't have been the same ones who took the diamond."

"What makes you say that?

"Lightning doesn't strike twice in the same place, does it?"

It actually could in the natural world—though not often. But it didn't seem likely here. "It seems stupid to return to the scene of the crime so soon."

She wrapped herself more tightly in the robe now as if getting cold. "But they also seemed awfully—slight—to be robbers."

"'Slight'?"

"More like young kids pulling a prank—but with guns.

School's out now, remember. So what were they really here for?"

I shook my head. "I think you need some sleep to rest that pretty little brain of yours."

She crooked her head. "Did it help yours?"

I chuckled. "I'm at least alert enough to take my turn watching the place now."

"I don't know if I can wind down after that episode."

I offered her the afghan I'd used. "Try."

She pulled it up to her neck while I helped her lie down. "Mmm," she said snuggling under it.

Maria emptied aspirins from the bottle into her palm and offered her the glass of water. I helped her with that. "You like bedroom now, Miss Randi?"

She smacked her lips together. "Thanks, Maria, but I don't want to move anytime soon." She mouthed "Thanks" to me, then despite her contention otherwise, her eyelids drooped. Within minutes, she'd fallen fast asleep. I was envious.

I replayed the alarm panel's video without the sound. They'd worn balaclavas so I could see only the back of their heads but I understood what Randi meant. They were too short and thin to be anybody we'd interviewed already, for one thing, but clearly demonstrated the agility of youth.

Even though Wade had been too free with information at that charity ball, who else could have known about Wade's extensive collection? These intruders didn't seem likely attendees. And they also seemed oblivious to the sophisticated alarm system here. Maybe they weren't the perps responsible for the diamond's theft.

I made another cursory inspection to ensure that the would-be invaders hadn't breached anything else before returning to the recliner, watching Randi breathe so contentedly but growing sleepier myself. By two o'clock I couldn't stop yawning so wide my eyes watered. I covered myself again with another colorful afghan, thankful Addy made such things in her spare time—and ended up dozing in spite of my efforts not to.

I awoke to Maria frying bacon and baking something with cinnamon and vanilla. That made Randi stir, too, stretching and yawning before she pried open her eyes, surprised when she saw me there near her.

"Am I dreaming," she said, "or is that a country breakfast I smell?"

"You're dreaming," I smiled as I approached her, "about a country breakfast that's for real."

She carefully rolled down the afghan from her front like the lid of a sardine can before she sat up, the robe parting, "Ow! I feel like I just did ten rounds with a briar patch—and the patch won."

"I thought you said you could handle pain."

"I *could* use a couple more pills."

"Yes, your majesty," I said, accommodating her since Maria had left the bottle there with the water. Then I checked her bandages.

"What are you looking at now?" she smirked.

Only one had come loose. I brushed a finger over an end, surprised it still stuck, then grinned. "Definitely a knock-out, that's for sure."

"Oh, you!" she said, balling her small fist at my arm as she struggled to get up with a groan. I helped her.

"Well, I guess, schweetheart," I said lamely imitating Bogie, "we slept together again like we did at the hospital at the end of the last case."

She twitched me another smile that made her lapse into another involuntary yawn. She closed the flopping flap of her robe, leaving it partly open so she wouldn't trip over the hem. "Not hardly, Nicky." She made the double negative sound charming.

When we padded into the kitchen, Randi barefoot, me in stocking feet, Maria showed off Randi's Levi jacket, skirt and blouse hanging on the back of the door to the utility room. "All ready, Miss Randi." The sunlight shone obliquely through the kitchen window portion that jutted out the back of the manor, reflections from the glass brightening something on the jacket. "I put back on your pin." She pointed to the dosimetry badge Randi had somehow left on from the last time she'd worn the Levi jacket, when we at last chanced onto the radioactive magic cape.

"Sorry, Maria," Randi said. "I forgot it was there." She seemed to think nothing of it but I stared at the tag and the color it bore.

It was while we were enjoying Maria's fried bacon and thick French toast, and I knew Maria had quite a culinary repertoire, that made me realize the Huntingtons had more treasures here than up in their Hall of Fame that the phone finally rang.

Wade's voice sounded gravelly still, showing he hadn't slept that well there in the hospital (who did?) when he apologized for "making" us stay the whole night. We assured him that it wasn't an imposition without going into the details. All I said was, "Maria took good care of us—" I winked at Maria who cast her eyes down like a shy little girl which made her dark cheeks rosier. "—and we took good care of her, too." Then I asked about Addy.

"I think she's almost out of the woods," he answered. "The swelling's down in her throat but she still can't quite swallow even water. They're hoping she can take some Jello by mid-day, maybe apple juice tonight."

That ubiquitous hospital Jello. What would modern medicine do without ground-up horses' hooves to pacify their patients?

"Peter's bringing me home later today so I can get some decent rest. Doctor's orders."

I hesitated to ask, still not sure who to blame for our unwanted visitors last night. "We've got our homework cut out for us today," I said, eyes connecting with Randi, "but we hope to check back with you for an update."

"I've got my fingers crossed they'll release her in time for Sunday's little 'do.'"

I had to ask, "How many people have you invited to this one?"

"You know Addy. She's got a buffet planned for sixty people afterwards. Seeing what happened before, I think there'll be a lot of food leftover."

"Not such a little event then," said Randi.

"I just hope she's up to it." A pause. "Hell, I hope *I* am!"

After Wade hung up, Randi sighed. "What people do for love."

"And rolling with the punches even after so long," I sighed. "It gives the rest of us hope."

"Not those of us," Randi remarked, an eyebrow lifting, "who already believe."

I quickly changed the subject. "Are you up to riffling through GEOS employees to look for possible prospects for those bungling burglars?"

"I could do with a little freshening up first," she said.

"Me, too," I said. "A shower back at our office where we can change into some clean underclothes—would that do the trick?"

"For me or you?" she said.

"Yes!" I smirked. "Except in your case, it's not going to be easy with all those scratches."

She hesitated. "You've covered the worst. I'll be careful. I have to be clean to feel 'human' again." By 'human,' of course, she meant 'woman.'

I nodded at her shoulder purse. "You've got more clothes in there?"

"Just what I changed out of. But being with you, I'm learning what it means to be prepared." She gave me a wily smile. "We can fit a lot more there than you can in those kangaroo pockets of yours."

"We'll stop back at the office then to clean up before we light out," I said.

"You bucking for Boss of the Year here?"

"Just for the year?"

"Maybe with a little humility thrown in?" she snickered.

Randi picked up the hanger with her jacket hung on the outside, squinting at the badge herself now, forehead knotted. "Then I'll buckle down for some serious internet surfing."

"You change in there?" said Maria, pointing to the utility room where Randi disappeared.

She bounded back in fluttering her clean skirt.

"This girl!" Maria laughed with a shake of her head. "Where you get this energy?"

Then Randi stopped as I pointed to her badge. "Did you take a good look at this thing?"

She squinted at it. "It's supposed to be green, isn't it?"

"It's *bright yellow* now. What exactly did you do in the Hall of Fame last night?"

"I made sure nothing else was missing. But I opened the case where the diamond had been and felt around the black velvet to see if the thieves left something behind we missed."

"We know the diamond had been irradiated to enhance its golden hue."

"Could the radiation linger this long after someone removed it?"

"Not enough to make the badge register like this." I tapped at my mustache.

"How am I ever going to get rid of the radiation then?"

"Hayley and Beanie both told us, remember, that it's easier than people think. Radiation lingers not so much in the air but on the *dust* in the air. You just have to wash the dust off with soap and water, including your hair."

"Who knew a shower could take care of so much? I'm even more anxious for one."

I hesitated now. "Those intruders may not have known we were here, but they knew something we didn't." My eyes widened—and now so did Randi's.

Randi breathed in sharply, gripping a hand on my forearm. "My God, Nicky? Could it be?"

"The diamond—" I started to say, eyes widening.

Then Randi voiced the obvious conclusion. "It's still *here!*"

I finished the thought. "And somewhere close by where it was!"

13

"We'll come back *very* soon," I assured Maria.

She'd heard our revelation and, though bewildered, knew we had some exploring to do upstairs. "I unlock rooms for you."

Randi and I looked at each other with this new dilemma.

"Should we stay and search first before Wade gets back?" said Randi.

"You need to wash up as soon as you can," I reminded her.

"So do you," she said. "You touched me. I may have contaminated you."

We looked at Maria. Would she be safe if the diamond were still here? I could tell Randi thought the same thing, but we didn't want to scare her. "You need to wash the rags and towel, and the afghan, too."

"I do this," Maria said.

"If we're on the right track here," I said, thinking aloud, "and our would-be intruders do work at GEOS, we might be able to nip this whole thing in the bud by confronting them there when they least expect it."

Randi elaborated for Maria's sake. "We don't know how long it'll take us to find it if it is still here."

I added only, "Keep the doors outside locked and the alarm on until we get back."

"Yes, Mr. Nick," she nodded. "And maybe I cook for you again?"

"We'll see," Randi smiled.

She tucked in her round chin, beaming. We'd clearly made more than one fan here at the manor.

Randi hadn't put her flats back on. She looked at me. "I don't like the feel without panty hose and I can't wear those quite yet. It looks like it's going to be another warm day. Is barefoot okay for now? At least until I can get home into some sandals."

I tried my hand at debonair insouciance. "Bare-legged, barefoot. All the same to me."

"I'll bet!" she smirked.

When we got back to the office by mid-morning, knowing it would take her longer to get cleaned up than I would, since she had to scrub herself well but be careful of her wounds, I let her go first.

I'd paid for a full bathroom as part of the tenant improvements there, thinking I might be busy enough to need it myself. Silly me. I *had* put in some late nights, but not very often before I saw the need to hire someone like Randi for organizational skills I lacked. But now I recognized its practicality for other reasons.

"You sure you can wait, Nicky?" she said, unbuttoning her blouse, looking around for a hanger.

"I've got some things to look up," I said, indicating the computer while I went to the guest closet for a plastic hanger, bringing it along with my brushed gray polyester robe, pointing to the hook on the other side of the bathroom door. She looked quizzically at the robe.

"I stayed late here sometimes checking credit card frauds before you came on the scene," I shrugged. "Dull work but it paid the bills."

"Sounds lonely."

"I thought a lot about beating the Maytag Man for the loneliest guy in town," I shrugged.

"So I saved the day just by showing up?"

"More than you know," I smiled.

"You want me to wear this out of the bathroom before I change?"

"It'll be too humid in there without opening the window before I take my shower. I didn't have room enough to include a dressing room."

"Okay," she said making the word longer than two syllables.

"Take your time. Don't forget to wash your hair, too, if Suave's okay."

"It'll do," she said, then quietly clicked the door shut, the plunger in the latch sticking again. I kept WD 40 in my bottom drawer for just such emergencies. I'd deal with it when my turn came.

I took the extra time for some preliminary "legwork" 21st century style on the internet. I noticed in the promotional blurb on the GEOS website that the institution had shifted to using "neodymium-doped yttrium aluminum garnet crystals" for most lasers they manufactured and tested for surgeries and other "cutting-edge applications"—whatever *that* meant. Why, then, had Sasha had that red crystal that Randi thought a ruby? I knew most laser technology today relied on synthetic rubies as they had since the very first lasers in 1959 and 1960. Real gems weren't necessary, not then anyway. So why would anyone there even be interested in a precious diamond this big?

Regarding the Kaslowskis, their website mentioned funding from such recognizable entities as the National Science Foundation, but also the more questionable Golden Order of the Dawn," "GOD," of all things! Its logo was a dragon with wings spread across the globe of a sun spiked with knife -sharp rays, silhouetting the creature. Donations, I guess, were donations though such a source seemed a little off-the-wall for legitimate scientific research.

"Nicky?" Randi's voice startled me out of this internet reverie. I turned around. She peeked her head out the door. "You have any more Bandaids here? Some came off."

I got up. "I forgot to tell you I keep a first-aid kit in the anteroom near your desk."

I returned to the door and offered her the whole box. She opened the door wider. She had wrapped herself only in the bath towel for now, her hair in long wet strands draping over her bare shoulders. "You're right. It's too icky in here for a robe. I'd like to use the other towel for my hair but then you wouldn't have a dry towel for yourself."

"Go on and use my hair dryer there then." I'd left it on the small counter next to the sink.

"I can do this in the office so you don't have to wait any longer. I'll just change outside while you're showering."

"I can wait a while longer."

"Where'd you get your patience?"

"You might have had something to do with it." But I'd learned a lot from my late wife, and before that, from my mother when we used to go shopping together during my teenage years in downtown Portland. We traded off priorities. If Angie wanted to sort through dress racks, she still wanted my opinion on what I liked when she tried them on. And I'd take my time browsing through books or records with her doing the same thing in a different section. Then we'd meet in the end over lunch and revel in our purchases.

Another plus here was enjoying how Randi's skin smelled of Dove soap, her hair of balsam, now that she was clean and wrapped only in that towel. She must have seen me brighten at all this, especially the latter, my face feeling hot as if I'd already showered.

"I'll just dry the worst off while I wait for the mirror to defog for you," she said, using one of my bristle brushes and turning on the dryer.

"When you change out here, just make sure the blinds are shut. You don't want to give our neighbors a sneak preview of your wares."

"'Wares,'" she giggled. "Like 'underwear'?"

Worse would be none at all when she removed the towel. I tried a throaty laugh. "Don't get any ideas!"

"No one can see much from a vacant parking lot anyway." But when she capered out, she took my suggestion, angling down the slats of the blinds, the morning sunlight barely filtering through. She pulled out another selection from the guest closet like a painting, replacing it with the one Maria had just laundered. How had she snuck so many in there already? She wasn't content with only one change of clothes per day? Still, I had to admit her strategy had assisted our cause already—with some lagniappes along the way for yours truly.

She saw me looking at her admiring this choice. "It's a pink Venus dress called 'Love Me Forever' that can sub as a swimsuit cover up. Rayon/polyester with summer straps. Plus a white jacket I added to slip on when it gets cool in the evening."

She didn't need to sell me but I joked back, "Sold!"

"Go on now," she tittered, "and get cleaned up so we can be a matched set!"

She began drying the rest of her hair in the full-length mirror I'd put up on the guest closet door for her, the towel loosening as she raised her arms.

Then I had to shut the bathroom door. The moisture on the mirror above the sink hadn't dissipated enough for me to shave. I let my clothes puddle to the floor, noting curiously that she'd washed and hung out her panties and bra on the lower rung of the double towel rack, a good precaution to rid all her clothes as well as her skin of radioactive dust. I should probably dry-clean my jacket and wash my clothes later, too, just to be safe though, my contamination had been "second-hand." Did that make a difference, though, to radiation?

The swirling blue script of "Friday" taunted me from her panties. I found some relief in its at least identifying the correct day today and remaining a sensuous reminder of her nickname.

I was oddly touched at her being so trusting. I hadn't realized I'd missed such intimacies I took so much for granted before losing Angie. It's really not just the person you miss as much as it is all the unexpected bonuses she brings along. I decided to shave in the shower instead with my wet/dry Norelco, using feel to make sure I didn't miss any spots. I usually turned the shower cool at the end, this time making it colder than usual, needing that more than ever.

I toweled dry though the steam lingered despite the ceiling fan which never worked quite as well as opening the window. I could do that later. I wanted to break the door slightly ajar to mitigate the humidity before putting back on my clothes so I wouldn't sweat but couldn't risk offending her. I'd have to use the hair dryer myself when she was finished but that never took me long.

Then I realized the foresight she'd shown washing her underwear. I hadn't thought ahead that much. For now I slipped back into them, hoping I wasn't being too forgiving of possible contamination. I applied my Stetson after shave balm on my face and some under my arms. Then I emerged feeling more refreshed, seeing that Randi had finished drying her hair and also donned the dress which hugged her maybe a little too well.

"You washed your underwear," I said. "Smart move."

"I couldn't take a chance not doing it. I'm more exposed than you were." She plucked at her straight strands, grimacing. "Broken ends and tangles. Wish I had my hot curlers."

"You're too critical," I said.

"Some conditioner would have helped," she pouted.

"It looks wonderful straight that way—like spun gold. My own Rapunzel."

"It's not *that* long!" She turned to look at herself in the mirror again. "You don't think I look better with my hair—bouncier?"

"You look perfect the way you are."

"You're not just saying that?"

"I say what I feel." Too much so sometimes. Maybe she was already learning that since she obviously did, too. "So you *did* have spare underwear in your purse then?"

She looked over her shoulder. "Not this time, like I said. I'm good—but not that good. Not yet."

"Then what are you wearing underneath?"

"Uh," she said, lips pursed, hips cocked to the side, hands fanning out the skirt portion girlishly, "nothing."

I gulped, then rasped out, "Nothing?"

She shook her head. "You don't mind, do you? With the bathroom window open and it getting warm again already, they should dry out in no time."

"Uh—" I stammered. "Well, we can't go out with you—

like that, can we?" This dress would barely cover her garter holster but it was snug enough that a breeze couldn't ruffle it the way one had Princess Kate revealing her very shapely "bum," as the British so quaintly put it.

"I think I'm safe enough in a dress that fits me this well." She looked back, a hand pressing at her chest self-consciously now to make sure she was right. "You can't really tell, can you? I mean, my breasts are fairly firm on their own, so unless I get too cold—"

I cleared my throat. "We don't really need to go into this, do we?"

"What are you saying? You certainly don't want me to put on—wet underwear, do you?"

I blanched. "Well, no."

"If you don't want to wait for my underthings to dry," she said, "I guess we should go back to my place for some fresh ones. I need to get some sandals anyway. It shouldn't cut into our day too much."

"We have to revisit GEOS at least," I said, glancing at my wristwatch. "I mean, once you scan the internet for employees there who could be our young intruders last night. Maybe we should consider Kaslowskis' students, too, who could be more devoted to their professors than they realize, especially if they mentioned something about the diamond on their camping trip. And it's imperative we get back to the Huntingtons before Wade shows. If it's there, it'll question his daughter's intentions."

"Whew, Nicky!" sighed Randi. "You want to do all that today? Isn't it more important to make sure the diamond's really there?"

"Bottom line, yes. It's only two more days until they renew their vows—if that's still on the docket. That means cramming these things in somehow if we're going to bring things to a close by then."

She fingered the side of her mouth. "First things first. My apartment for undies and sandals. I've got another set of the weekday panties. They're Barely There, my favorite because you can't see the lines across here." She demonstrated by pulling the dress across her hips though she probably shouldn't have done that then as tight as the dress already was. I gulped. But how my mind took wing!

I almost choked on my saliva. I finally stated the obvious. "Sometimes, Randi, you share too much."

"And you don't?" she said. "I thought you preferred us honest with each other. Most people are so phony."

"That's what makes our job so hard," I sighed. "But yes, I guess, I prefer us honest. We have to trust each other above all."

She paused a moment. "I don't tell you...everything Nicky, though I'd like to. There's something I'm dying to tell you." She wriggled a little, snapping at one of the straps, so that it fit better on the top. "I've got to tell you soon or I'll burst."

I hesitated, uncertain what she could mean. "I can wait until you're ready."

"Well, let's get to it then," she smiled.

"To what?" I said, still puzzled at this disclosure that didn't seem to be one. She could make my mind spin like a centrifuge.

"I'll take my underthings home, silly," she said, "and dry them there while I put on my spare pair and find some decent sandals."

I stared at her as she returned my glance. "Shouldn't you stop at your place to change your underwear, too? Can't be too careful since I may have exposed you to too much." No kidding, I thought. "Don't you want to feel fresh all over? You smell so nice and everything. I love that fragrance."

"Stetson," I said.

"My own real-live cowboy?" she smirked.

I tipped my invisible cowboy hat. "Not exactly, ma'am."

She giggled again. "So time to saddle up?"

"You got it, darlin'."

She couldn't stop giggling. "I'll be lickity split, you'll see."

"It'll be a relief," I said with a long sigh, "to keep my private secretary 'private.'"

"You're so sweet, Nicky." She then pecked me on my cheek, sniffing me deeply as she gathered up her underthings from the bathroom, shouldering her purse and following me out the door until I made sure she preceded me, in this case an absolute necessity.

She noticed, of course, putting a different spin on my earlier remark. "Smart move. I'd never be able to catch you if you had a heart attack looking back up at me!"

"You can be a little imp sometimes, you know?"

She suppressed another giggle. "Only one of my many talents."

"So I'm learning."

She acted quite demure in the car on the way to her apartment, even though the dress was quite tight and very short so that I could hear her thighs squeak across the leather.

"Don't worry," she assured me. "You won't see anything but my bunged-up legs."

"Just making sure."

"Right," she said, drawing out the word like a summer breeze.

"We weren't exactly Fred and Ginger out there on the lawn last night."

She gave a hearty laugh. "You call that dancing?"

"We've definitely got work to do," I smiled back, "on this partner part."

Randi's apartment complex was located on the southern side of Ashborough opposite Shute Park, a part of Ashborough that had gone downhill in the '80's. I didn't want to call that to her attention. Maybe she already knew.

"Don't worry, by the way," she smiled back coyly. "I'm on the ground floor, although it's a townhouse with the bedroom upstairs."

Well, I was safe as long as I didn't watch her climb the stairs then. I made a show of swiping the back of my hand across my forehead. She smiled even more broadly at that before unlocking the front door in a small alcove shared by the opposite unit, then making a beeline to the machines stacked in a louvered closet where she placed her underthings in a netted lingerie bag before shoving them into the dryer. "Want some coffee while you wait?"

I shook my head. "It'll go right through me."

"Okay. I'll be back in a flash." She giggled again.

"You're incorrigible," I muttered.

She came back down less than fifteen minutes later—I had to check my watch because I had trouble believing it—snapping at the elastic band of her panties through the skirt portion and adjusting one of the straps to her bra so it didn't show out the wider straps of the dress. "'Ready Randi'—right? Now your turn!"

So I took her back to my place. This was the first time she'd been there since she'd had the urge to clean the inside of my van for our first major "stake-out" when I hadn't let her see anything but the inside of my garage, afraid she'd start on the inside of the house which would have been like taking on the Augean stables. "You're actually going to invite me into your den of iniquity?"

"You've been reading too many detective stories again," I chuckled. "Hardly 'iniquity'—though 'infamy' probably comes closer to the truth. Just don't touch anything while you're waiting. I know where everything is—or, more likely, *isn't*."

"You know me," she said.

"That's why I said that!"

"Even though I've got that special woman's touch? Almost like a fairy godmother."

I just shook my head. "Not today, sweetie. We're burning daylight."

"Is that more cowboy talk?"

“Well, sort of.” Although John Wayne had popularized it, the phrase actually dated back to Shakespeare. This didn’t seem the right time to share that.

We pulled into the garage, though I left the door up while we got out and entered the utility room, making our way to the open kitchen where I sat her down. “Like you said, back—but like the Flash.”

She didn’t catch the comic book twist, snickering through her nose at what she took to be me reprising her remark. “They call my garter holster a ‘flash-bang,’ you know. Flash the target—then bang!”

“I’ll never beat you at that game.”

“At least we’ve got that settled.” She gave me a flirty squint pulling down her skirt again though to me that only called even more attention to her damaged but still shapely legs.

These moments of persiflage sometimes teetered on dangerous territory.

I returned shortly splaying my arms out like a rodeo cowboy that had just tied up his calf in record time. “Happy now?”

“See what a difference clean underwear makes?” she beamed back.

Better than none at all, I was thinking. I nodded at the more prominent Bandaids on her knees. “You can certainly play the sympathy card now to win over prospective suspects now.”

“They’re going to think you’re some protector of ladies.”

I paled a moment. These were different times. “I didn’t

think of that."

"Don't worry, Nicky," she said, placing a hand on my arm as we returned to the van. "I'll make it clear these were earned in the line of duty."

I sighed. "That's my girl."

That inspired another bright smile. We returned to the office where Randi now explored possibilities on the internet, trolling Facebook with more patience than I had. "Sam Dekker and Elaine Schatz, right?"

"You remembered those students' names," I said, "while you were busy surviving those glass chips?"

"Maybe the pain branded them into my memory," she smirked. But she did find a Sam Dekker and an Elaine Schatz in the Beaverton area, their Facebook sites acknowledging they were both archeology graduate students at the U of O. "These must be the ones."

She motioned me over to the laptop at her front desk. "That was fast."

She sat back to make room for me to look. "Not much stays private anymore, Nicky. But they aren't likely to be our intruders." I examined the portraits they'd posted. Sam Dekker had much blonder hair than his mentor with dark blue eyes and a square jaw plus a stocky build, his shoulders broad like an ox. Elaine Schatz's oval face sported lavender eyes like Elizabeth Taylor with an equally black mane of hair so curly it seemed naturally frizzed. They both looked like they worked out boasting very tanned faces, a tribute to their penchant for the outdoor life.

"They haven't got the same body types, that's for sure," I

said.

"Girls usually have a different gait than guys—even when running. The way we hold our arms for one thing unless they're marathon runners. But come to think of it, those intruders did look stringy but athletic enough in their own right. The guy loped like he had strong legs. And the girl, the shorter, thinner shadow, did pump her arms like a professional runner."

"You could tell all that from where we fell?"

"I'd seen them full-on in the floodlight first as you were waking up. But yeah, I could see that until their shadows faded into the night."

Normally eyewitnesses to crimes were notoriously unreliable despite what TV and movies showed. Moments of disaster always threw everybody off, except trained professionals, sometimes even them, too. Randi seemed confident enough here, though, that I trusted her judgment.

"The lab assistants at GEOS we saw through the window," Randi added, "looked like young Orientals—more like the build of our Ninja wannabees."

We thought checking for a list of employees at GEOS first from its website might help us isolate possibilities. I hadn't noticed before the prominent slogan beneath its logo of the lightning bolt breaking apart the "O" of the Earth: "Drawing from the planet to power our future." Randi scrolled past the tabs on its history—it originated in 1995 so was relatively new on the high-tech scene, and hoped to access information on more than its founders and the staff. But we hit a wall when it came to the assistants. She sat back with resignation. "That's the pits."

So we had to head off to revisit GEOS after all in nearby Beaverton. Ashley at the receptionist desk couldn't help us, but the guards on duty there permitted us to access the personnel files once we took the tack of saying we were investigating on-the-job safety records and insurance liabilities at the request of our client, worried about how a friendship with two of their research staff members might have compromised her family's privacy. It struck the right chord with the security guards though they kept the password to themselves. Sometimes paranoid times ironically helped us lift the lid of secrecy just enough.

That's how we discovered Dr. Arkov had a female lab assistant, Dr. Borishnikol a male—boy, girl, boy, girl even in the workplace. It made some sense. Despite the sexual tension—or maybe because of it—I could attest to the fact that men and women sometimes worked better together than the same sex even while I was a detective at Nohomish County though I was never partnered with a woman except when training rookies. It wasn't just a question of diversity. As long as people respected the boundaries of intimacy, relationships benefited because each gender was attuned to different priorities, one seeing what the other might not. Such varied perspectives could aid in observing sensitive experiments here, too.

No photos still but the names stood out. "James and Amiko Asaki."

"Married," whispered Randi, "or brother and sister?" But she couldn't find any more data. "If everything else is so confidential, I doubt they'll be on Facebook. But I'll check later on my laptop."

We returned to Ashley and asked if they were in today and accessible for questioning. In person interviews would still be best.

"They both called in sick today," said Ashley.

"Interesting," I said as we backed away.

Then Randi excused herself, saying she had to go to the bathroom. I was a little surprised since she hadn't drunk any coffee or water since breakfast. Neither had we had time for lunch yet because of the showers and the stopovers. I looked around while I waited for her, wondering if we shouldn't try to check in with the research physicists again instead. I asked Ashley whether they were available.

"Not today," she said, checking the monitor, not looking me in the eye. "They're engaged in a delicate project in the basement that will keep them incommunicado all day. That's all I know." Had the good doctors instructed her not to allow us further access to them after our first awkward encounter? Or could they be looking out for their assistants now, too?

When Randi returned—it had been a long twenty minutes—I said, "You okay?"

She nodded, also avoiding my eyes. "Uh-huh." But then she wagged her head towards the front door.

"You were gone so long, I began to worry." Residual effects from the glass chips?

She held her thumb and forefinger up. "So you missed me just a little?"

"Just a little," I said with the glimmer of a smile, not wanting it to go to her head. "I was hoping we could see somebody while we were here so it wouldn't be a wasted trip."

"Outside," she said. We made our way back to the van when she confessed, "I've been busy sneaking in some secret sleuthing of my own."

I widened my eyes. "You looked for our mysterious Mikel and Sasha or the Asakis?"

She shook her head no. "I checked with Finance like Dr. Arkov suggested. The twenty grand to our dear Mena came personally from Manfred Duncan, head of Project Thunderstone—which Doctors Arkov and Barishnikol are spearheading!"

I jerked my head back. "How did you find that out—without a security badge?"

"Girl talk!" she confided. "I showed the girl at the front desk in Finance my card and said I needed to find out for my client—but that I also needed a Tampon and didn't see a dispenser in the ladies' restroom. She felt sorry for me, especially with my legs looking like this, which I made sure she noticed, then gave me a fresh one from her purse!"

I shook my head now. "You're making yourself indispensable again."

"Good!" she said, touching the back of my hand, scrunching up her body with delight. "I did ask about the Asakis being there, too, but no soap. Unlisted phone number. We'll have to try a different tack."

"So phantoms?"

"For now. We might need help from Beanie and friends."

"It's almost the weekend. I'm not sure they'll be available in time before Sunday."

"Do I still get a reward—like something to eat?"

On our way to some fast food place that she wouldn't reject out of hand, I mulled over that word aloud. "Thunderstone."

"A made-up word or is it another kind of gem they're looking into?"

"I think it's an obsolete term for lightning, but it could refer to fulgurite, a stone that's caused when a lightning bolt strikes sand, now also by the detonation of a nuclear device."

"Oh, my God, Nicky. What's GEOS *doing* behind closed doors, anyway?"

"Scary to think," I said. The website had boasted that government funding was its lifeblood. That usually meant the military.

"But their motto makes them sound like they're interested in improving the world by relying on natural resources."

"A lot of scientists start out with the best of intentions. I'm beginning to wonder if we'll ever get the truth out of these modern-day sorcerers along with their absentee apprentices—if these disciples really *are* our missing miscreants."

"I love the way you talk, Nicky!" Then Randi added something much more ominous. "They may just come out of the woodwork and track us down instead, Nicky, if we find what we think is waiting for us back at the manor."

"You do sometimes flirt too much with disaster, Randi," I said, surprised she'd gotten away with her little deception this time. "That receptionist could have turned you in, and then they'd never have let us stay free agents!"

"But she didn't," she said with that coy smile. Talk about gender bending the rules! "Can I help it if I'm getting good at subterfuge?"

I smirked at her word. She was even beginning to sound more like a spy now! Or was this due to her weakness for detective stories—or crossword puzzles? I glanced at my watch. It was already past one o'clock. I decided to chance pulling into a Burger King in Orenco Village off Cornell Road on our way back to Ashborough.

Randi rolled her eyes. "Oh, Nicky, no!"

"Even for a quickie lunch?" I said. "I'm just trying to be an equal opportunity fast-foodie. You can find healthier offerings here now, too."

She sulked, locking arms together over her chest.

I persisted. "I don't know how long it'll take us to scour the manor when we get there. Something now's better than skipping lunch altogether, isn't it? We won't just eat in the car."

"I guess you're right," she relented with a side glance. "That's a partial victory for my side. Besides, I could use the pit stop."

"See? There's something good even in settling for less right now. Once we know for sure whether our hunch is right about the stash at the manor, we'll have time to enjoy a decent meal."

"If we're not too busy circling the wagons," she reminded me.

"It's not like you to sound so doom and gloom."

She shuddered. "Thinking about what GEOS is really doing gives me the willies."

When we passed through the glass doors, she headed straight for the rest room, looking back at me. "Don't you have to go yet?"

I shrugged, placating by following her, entering the men's room then waiting outside her door until she re-emerged later than I thought normal.

I knitted my forehead at her before we walked to the order counter. "Aren't you going more than usual?"

She looked askance. "I didn't really go there at GEOS. It was just a ruse."

"So it's not—well—" I nodded at her pelvis as she raised her own eyebrows so I decided to be more specific. "—your time or anything?"

"Nicky! I wouldn't have gone without panties earlier if that were the case. I'm not about to tempt fate *that* much."

I felt the blood drain from my face again. This was getting to be my signature reaction to her candor. Better than blushing, I suppose. I looked around to make sure no one had heard that. I was worried because my late wife had experienced a similar bout of frequent urination. But Randi had certainly been convincing enough with me so I could see why that girl at Finance believed her. "I was just afraid you might have something like a bladder infection."

She recoiled, her mouth agape. "Nicky! Girls don't usually get that kind of thing unless they've gone swimming in dirty water or—you know—been intimate—with a new guy."

I backed off. "Sorry. I just don't want anything bad to happen to you if I can help it."

She softened at that. "You should know by now I'd tell you the truth."

Trying to appease her more to make up for this faux pas, I ordered a chicken burger while she chose a chicken salad along with coffee finally. It would help keep me alert after a somewhat fitful night's sleep, though she seemed to sleep well enough even laid out on that sofa. Though they smelled tempting, I skipped the fries.

"Thanks, sweetie," I told her, "for something to tide us over. I promise you there'll be a much better carrot at the end of the stick from now on."

Her eyes twinkled as she stabbed the plastic fork at her salad. "That's sounding like an old refrain."

The only thought I broached about what lay ahead of us was one remark towards the end of our lunch, such as it was. "Have you thought about the implications if we do find what we're looking for?"

"Have you—if we don't?"

We didn't even begin to know the half of it.

14

When we parked in front of the manor and got out, the afternoon sky was already turning fiery, the recurring cirrus clouds looking themselves like wind-blown corn silk. Maria rubbered a broad smile our way when we walked into the kitchen as if she'd expected us more than the master of the house who still, thankfully, hadn't shown. "Miss Randi, you change clothes *again*?"

"We had some people to see that required it," I said in her defense. "But you know Randi."

"So," Maria said, "you stay for dinner again?"

"We'll know better after our search upstairs," I told her.

"I have keys," she said, jingling them in her apron's pocket.

Randi said, though, "What's keeping Wade?"

Maria shrugged. "No call."

I suggested we start with Mena's old room. "Sometime

Miss Mena—she stay when she has the problem. They keep it the way she leave it." She didn't elaborate on the "problem," the vagueness dangling in air like a Damoclean sword.

"Recently?" I said.

"Not so much now—but sometime," said Maria.

When we reached the bedroom at the end of the display cases next to the large master suite, she slid the key into the lock with some difficulty before shoving the door open. "It stick sometime."

A mustiness seeped out. She wrinkled up her face as she backed away to let us in. "I wish they let me clean and air out, but no dice." The idiom seemed odd coming from her but sweet, showing she was trying to speak more colloquially.

"We'll do our best to keep everything as is," Randi promised.

"You take the time," she said.

I had to add, "We'll keep this our little secret, okay?"

"Is good," she nodded. "I start the dinner anyhow. Is meatloaf today. Special recipe. You like, too, I bet. Is Mr. Wade favorite."

Randi cast a look back at her as she left.

I checked my watch. It was almost three o'clock already. Wade was really late.

"Clever, Nicky," she whispered. "You made her our lookout without telling her that."

I gave her a thumbs-up.

"Meatloaf," Randi clucked, nose wrinkling more because of the room's staleness. "It was usually an excuse for Mom to throw together a week's worth of leftovers."

"Not at our house," I said absently as I scanned the walls. "Mom mixed ground pork with beef and stale Rhodes bread she wetted down before mixing in milk, an egg plus garlic, onions and Italian seasoning—plus a dash of Worchester sauce."

"You remember the recipe in that much detail?"

"One of my favorites, too," I smiled.

"A little early to start preparing dinner, isn't it?" she said.

"She obviously likes fussing in the kitchen to keep busy, itching to get her hands on these rooms, you notice."

The bedroom seemed a dusty shrine to Mena's teenage years. Lacey curtains with flounces rippled slightly from the mostly closed floor vent, looking almost like old-fashioned parted bloomers the way they framed either side of the sash. To the left lay a daybed with a puffy pink floral quilt flush against the wall featuring an ugly worn Cabbage Patch doll and a stuffed pillow in the shape of a rainbow-colored snake. Randi picked it up with thumb and forefinger and dropped it back. "Not exactly a cuddly teddy bear."

"To each her own," I shrugged.

At the right of the bed's brass fretted headwork sat a small secretariat roll-top desk crammed into the corner, a simple worn green secretary chair in between its spindly oak legs.

The other wall to our right featured an ornate white vanity table dotted with the requisite bottles of perfume, make-up and even a pink Princess phone the Huntingtons must have saved from their early days for their daughter. That gave me an idea. I felt in my pocket to see if I still had what I'd kept from our last time with Beanie and friends when they equipped us with surplus surveillance equipment.

Beside the vanity rose a cabinet trimmed with pink gingerbread beside the oval mirror that spanned the low desktop where a white settee with gold filigree perched. A picture of Mena in a cap and gown beside just her father stood angled open in the center. The other half of the clamshell frame showed her mother and father posed like Bonnie and Clyde in front of a Harley Davidson with Wade dressed in bell bottom brown corduroy pants and Addy decked out in a short paisley dress with long straight dark hair as if the hippie costumes were afterthoughts. It seemed fitting now that he'd gone into the "natural bread" market, a spin-off of communal co-op days from that era that became passé as I grew up during the disco craze but had led into the artisan bread fad today.

The wall on the hall side held a narrow white set of dresser drawers, knobs tinged with gold. Behind the door as we came into the center of the room hung a movie poster of Patrick Swayze behind Jennifer Gray, her arm cocked about his face with her staring up at him doe-eyed, from "Dirty Dancing." Beneath it a sewing machine table jutted out like an intrusion, a wicker basket on the floor stuffed with tangled yarn, remnants of unfinished projects.

Randi and I shared a confused glance that said we were thinking the same thing: Mena's childhood "things" didn't seem to jibe with the "Lady Vandemere" we'd met. Princess

-like, perhaps, but royalty American-style and much more "Disneyized."

Randi started opening and closing the drawers and cabinet doors to the vanity before sliding up the roll-top desk where papers were strewn everywhere as if it had become a forlorn trash bin instead. Meanwhile, I rummaged through the chiffonier trying to ignore the old man staring back at me from its oval mirror overhead. Too many mirrors for my taste, though I guess not for a girl reaching womanhood, or maybe a woman sometimes wistful about girlhood now gone. One of the drawers I plied through in the chest still had piles of her slips and underthings from what looked like her teenage years—colored bras and garish panty sets, including a leopard skin imitation that seemed incongruous, black leggings and a set of white ones along with ballet slippers. As much as I fingered through these neat piles, I found nothing hidden but packets of sachet—though I needed Randi to tell me what they were.

I finally had to voice my concern. "Do we know what we're looking for?"

"A special 'girl cache,'" said Randi. "You know, where girls are apt to stash diaries and private things away from the prying eyes of parents?"

"Your specialty, I'm afraid, not mine," I said, mouth pinched to the side. "But even when computers began creeping into teenagers' lives?"

"Girl diaries never go out of style, Nicky. I mean, I kept one, too."

"Maybe her secret stash," I wondered, "is 'hidden' in

plain sight? Like what we found at the end of our last case."

She paused with her combing through everything to stare at me. "Maybe so. We might be looking too hard."

We studied the room's walls then and even the floor despite its being fully carpeted in tufted off-white, looking for suspicious seams or cracks. I even considered the bordered wallpaper garlanded with pink and red roses all the way around the bedroom at the top of the walls though it was too narrow to hide anything substantial. "What's wrong with just secreting it away in one of these drawers?" I said in frustration. "She has plenty."

"First place a parent would search," said Randi though that hadn't stopped her so far.

We heard a clattering outside the door before it swung ajar. "Mr. Wade—he just call. Peter bring home now. Miss Mena come when she can. In meantime you come down for tapas and the wine?"

I glanced again at my watch. I couldn't believe we'd spent over an hour already scouring this one room. But Randi and I looked at each other with a telling stare. I could see she didn't want to hurt Maria's feeling. I'd gotten the impression she was hoping for a more private dinner just the two of us.

"A sweet offer, Maria," said Randi. "We've got—other plans I think. But those hors d'oeuvres sound great." Her eyes flicked to mine. She was offering a temporary compromise.

"We're almost done," I said uncertainly.

It was enough to satisfy Maria who turned with only one

parting remark. "Tapas best hot." We heard her shuffle down the stairs.

"But we haven't found anything yet, Nicky."

"Maybe getting away from it for a while will help. We're not giving up. There's got to be some sign somewhere here."

We tried to put things back in order as much as possible figuring Mena would stay over before the Sunday ceremony since the church was nearer here than her home. Her mother would be too weak if the doctor let her come home tomorrow anyway and could use the help.

Randi grabbed hands on her hip, surveying the room one more time, then shrugged at me before I slowly closed the door. I glanced at the empty case on the other side almost at eye level, thinking, while Randi slid her arm through the crook in mine, her eyebrows knitted together so tightly they seemed a ghostly white under the canned lights of the hall as we left.

Maria poured out glasses of a blended red wine that we sipped after clinking the rims. She opened the oven and slid out the wedge-shaped pieces of pita bread she'd browned until crisp for dipping into the salsa dish sitting on the center island. With a spatula, she scooped them off the parchment paper covering the cookie sheet, placing them on torn paper grocery bags for draining off what smelled like olive oil. I reached for one to sample, dabbing the tip into the sauce.

"Is hot," warned Maria.

I munched the tip of the wedge tentatively, letting it loll on my tongue, tasting the salt but opening my mouth wide in a vain effort to cool it off. I jumped the gun as I often did with pizza when it smelled too good to wait. "You got that right." The words were garbled while my tongue recovered but Randi understood and smiled. So much for the patience she'd lauded earlier.

Then suddenly Randi and I locked eyes that flicked up from her having covered the cookie tray with parchment.

I snapped my fingers at the one obvious thing we'd missed in overturning Mena's room.

"*Covers*," Randi exclaimed.

We clicked the base of the goblets down on the granite tile. "We forgot something upstairs," I told Maria.

Maria looked at us warily. "I keep tapas warm?"

"We'll be right back!" Randi said breathlessly.

"You young ones! Always in the hurry." But she offered a slanted smile.

We scrambled up the stairs, bursting back into the room. I checked the corners of the "Dirty Dancing" poster. The bottom ones curled up slightly. The thumbtacks left many holes in the wall as we let it scroll up so we could better scrutinize the wall for possible seams. Then we saw it plain as day.

"Just like in 'The Shawshank Redemption,'" I breathed. "That might even have inspired her. What better place for a cubby hole than behind a movie poster—and in back of the display cases?"

"Her password 'rabbit hole'!" she said. "We should kick ourselves."

"Me first!" I joked. "I read the story and saw the film!"

Carefully we unhooked the entire movie photo placing it

on the daybed, making note of the bigger pinholes the thumbtacks made. The lines of the small drawer had been cleverly concealed with paint feathered from the off-white wall paint. I used the pocket knife I'd inherited from Dad that he'd carried with him everywhere and kept ultra-sharp. I'd saved it in his memory, using the blade now to pry open what I could without making it too obvious. "This wall must have used two by sixes instead of regular studs to be so thick," I said. "Wade did tell us he made an extra effort to soundproof the place."

"And that backing reinforced support for the cases on the other side," Randi added.

Despite my care, sheetrock pieces crumbled to the floor. "Picking locks would have been easier."

"You need a woman's touch." She was in fact more persevering at prying the slot apart, tongue at the side of her lips like a little girl.

A tick-click. She'd unlatched a hasp. With care she jiggled the front of the drawer loose, withdrawing it slowly like a safety deposit box but much shallower. Mena had gone to a lot of bother to make this hideaway with the care of a craftsman. But then she *had* majored in arts and craft at college, hadn't she? The tray tilted so that Randi almost dropped it. I held a hand beneath to steady it. The hall light flashed through from the side where the display cases lay.

Then we lifted the lid of the tray. Inside, placed sideways, was a padded red book—as Randi had predicted—embossed with gold letters blaring, "My Diary." It bore a thin layer of dust with fingerprints smudged at the clasp. I held it in my palm draped with my handkerchief.

Something else lay clumped in a purple velvet draw purse that Randi picked up while I held the diary. She loosened the top draw string, releasing a veritable genie of beauty that made us both gasp.

In the dimness of that bedroom's globed ceiling light, it shimmered with an ethereal glory from the myriad facets of its rose cut, splaying out numerous golden spikes over our faces, a scarlet stream firing from its center in a thin beam like the laser atop Vegas' Luxor pyramid.

She said this in a desperate whisper. "Not a carrot at the end of the stick, Nicky—but *carats!*"

"Ninety-nine of them," I breathed out.

The Golden Diamond of Kolimar!!

15

"My God, Nicky," Randi went on, cupping it like the Holy Grail—which to us it was. "I've never seen anything so beautiful!"

"It sparkles as if it harbors a fire of its own," I said, breathless as well.

She looked up momentarily at me, then back down, obviously enthralled and frightened at the same time. "Is it because it was 'irradiated'?"

"Sari knew from photos that it bore this rose cut, traditional for centuries. That makes them shine with a special splendor that's hard to top."

"It's—*perfect*." Well, we didn't really know that for a fact. She was letting her natural exuberance overwhelm her again. I couldn't blame her.

I couldn't refute its obvious enchantment but felt obliged to bring us back down to earth. "A diamond in the rough isn't very spectacular, you know." I was remembering bits coming back from the insurance adjuster and what she'd showed me on her computer before she began her research into the worth of this jewel. "In its natural state in rock, it's a milky white, kind of like dirty quartz."

"It's warm," breathed Randi. "I can feel it through the velvet." She tore herself away from staring so intently. "Like the magic cape?"

I just shook my head, reaching out with my free hand that hovered over hers. Even without touching it, I could sense the heat it gave off.

"Is it even safe to hold?" she said.

"Irradiating just releases an intrinsic brightness even if it's an artificial way experts now condemn. But this seems—beyond natural." We moved to the vanity table where I encouraged her to set it down half in, half out of its small sack.

"So how are we supposed to handle this now, Nicky? Mena—and maybe her husband—are obviously behind 'stealing' this diamond. But if it's still here in her parents' house, has a crime actually been committed?"

"Technically, no," I offered. "Not until it leaves the house. But there's also no precedent for this."

"But the intruders, Nicky!" whispered Randi. "Somehow they—*knew!*"

"Did Mena mean to collect on the insurance," I said, "or was she about to give it up to others for that measly twenty grand when she could have asked for the moon? Something else must still be pending."

"Right now we're the only ones who know about any of

this," she said. "But we still don't know the whole story."

I brushed a finger at my mustache, remembering what I'd said before. "It's still being written."

"Can't we just confront her before it changes hands?"

"She's technically our client, sweetie," I said. "We have to let this play out, but be there to catch her if she falls too far."

Randi wasn't letting loose of the diamond. "Has she filched on the deal with GEOS? Did the Kaslowskis strike their own bargain with her? What if that organization 'G.O.D.' pushed them into this?" Then she realized what I'd already surmised. "She's about to double-cross *somebody*. We need to find out what arrangements Mena's made, and who the real enemies are, then make sure she, or we, aren't caught in the crossfire."

She was on a roll. I couldn't add a word.

"One thing's for sure," Randi concluded. "Whoever the intruders were last night, they represent an 'injured party.' They were here to set things right, for them."

She used the handkerchief I held the diary in to slide it onto a space she made on the opened rolltop desk, then gently peeled open pages starting with the back first, the way my mother used to read her movie magazines. "Maybe there's a hint somewhere in this that will help us understand some of what motivated her to put all this in motion. The last entry's dated six years ago, so before she got married."

"For now," I said, looking at the poster we'd laid across the daybed, "we'd better put everything back the way it was, as much as possible."

Randi glanced over at the diamond that was still casting its web-like charm all over the room, dazzling our eyes even from where it lay. "The diamond, too?"

"We're the most disinterested parties in this little drama, but now it's about to open up a Pandora's box. And we need to see what's inside."

Randi gazed at it longingly. "How do we keep the treasure safe—and let it go at the same time?"

I raised an arm like the Tin Man when he says they should erect a statue to him. "We represent the law like the knights of old, the defenders of the realm, the voice of reason—"

"Then why are you going on and on about it?"

She had me there. I was trying to convince myself. "We're still the arbiters of what's just for all concerned. The rightful owners still need to have it returned."

"So we're slogging through that swampy 'gray area' again," she declared.

"It's best for now that Mena doesn't know we know. We have to put it back and let her go through with some of whatever she's planned, but somehow keep it, and her, safe."

"'Safe,' Nicky? That's not an easy word to toss around right now."

"We've got more pressing homework to take care of first." I pointed at the diary.

Randi, though, was one step ahead of me already, snapping pictures with her iphone she'd fished out of her purse. "We can study these later with no one the wiser—and maybe figure out what drove her to this."

"Good thinking. But I'm not sure entries that old will help us understand what possessed Mena to pull a stunt like this today. Her husband must be in cahoots with her. And it's not simply greed. There's no way she could fence this big of a diamond—but lending it out for pennies like a library? That makes no sense either."

Then we heard a ruckus coming from below. "You two ready?" Maria shouted up.

"We'll be down in a sec," Randi answered.

We could tell Maria was now scurrying to the front door followed by a rustling of shambling feet. "You home at last!" she cried.

Randi hunched down, lips close to my ear. "It sounds like Peter's helping Wade in." Then a woman's voice broke in. It couldn't be Addy's. Not this soon.

Randi uttered it in a whisper first even as the truth registered with me, too. "*Mena!*"

We had to hustle to get everything back looking as undisturbed as possible—and before anyone knew what we'd done. Now I understood what burglars felt like when they'd been interrupted in the middle of a botched theft. We shoved the diamond back into its velvet pouch, hastily arranging the diary back sideways next to it into the small drawer. The handkerchief helped. Only Mena's fingerprints showed.

"She's still bound to know, Nicky, *something*."

Randi licked her fingers, then tried to smear some of the plaster over the seams of the door. It was the best we could do in the short time we had.

"She might think," I offered, "she left the signs herself when she slid the diamond into this hidey hole the night of the dinner." Even if she suspected something more, it might give her second thoughts about going through with whatever arrangement she'd concocted.

Footsteps slowly but methodically mounted the stairs.

We flattened the poster back into place as best we could, she taking the lower half, me the upper, and jabbed the thumbtacks into the holes we thought the deepest.

I palmed some of the puckers away as did Randi. "Thank you," I whispered, tapping at their faces, "Patrick and Jennifer!"

We spun around lurching for the door, locking it first before clicking it as quietly shut as we could. Then trying not to look too guilty, we scrambled to the top of the stairs to see who was coming up to get us.

"Wade and Peter!" I breathed out, trying to hide my relief. "We were just checking your collection again."

"Glad to be home," Wade sighed. "Maria's anxious for you to rejoin her. The meatloaf's almost done."

At the base of the stairs, Mena stared up. "I got off early from work," she said, "but Mother's not being released until tomorrow now." We came down behind Peter still holding up Wade's slouched frame. But then she gaped at us. "What are you two doing here?"

I picked the most credible excuse. "Your father felt safer having us check back here while he was away."

Mena narrowed her eyes at us, second nature to her, I guess.

"Maria," Randi said, "was happy to have the company last night."

A good thing Randi added that. It helped ease Mena's doubt. Wade gazed longingly at the liquor cabinet with a crooked smile. "I could sure use a drink." He glanced back at us as Peter marched him to his favorite easy chair where I'd slept, his daughter trailing after. "And some company, too."

I indicated the center island. "Maria's already poured our wine to go with her tapas."

"You don't want to overdo, Dad," Mena reproved. "You've got a lot ahead of you once Mother comes home tomorrow if she goes through with this thing on Sunday."

"I know what I'm doing," he assured her, bristling a bit. The fatigue showed in his voice.

Mena had a faraway look in her eyes. "I just hope everything comes off as planned."

I didn't want to look over at Randi or we might give ourselves away, suspecting she wasn't thinking of the ceremony.

"It's going to be a big day," I agreed, covering all bases.

Maria poured him his drink at the kitchen bar but Mena, acting unusually unctuous, delivered it to him where he sat.

"You don't need to stay tonight, honey," he said to his daughter. "But tomorrow would be nice. Maybe like old times?"

"I can go home after dinner tonight then," she said, eyes deep-set looking almost bruised with what must have been lack of sleep. She looked over at Maria. "Maybe I could take a doggy bag back to Matt?"

Maria smiled. "I do this, Miss Mena." Then she turned towards Randi and me as we finished our wine and took another couple of her tapas. "You stay for dinner, too?"

"You're a dear for asking us again," Randi answered, "but we have something planned, don't we, Nicky?"

I shrugged sheepishly. "I've promised to make things up to her for our overnight stay here last night," I said.

"I'm really pretty easy," Randi grinned.

"Ho!" said Wade. "If only that were true with women!"

"Well," I said, "I for one believe her."

"Oh, boy," said Wade. "You're a goner, Nick—though I don't blame you. Addy had me in the palm of her hand from the time we met at a Three Dog Night concert!"

"It doesn't take much, does it?" I grinned as Randi almost danced me to the door.

He drank down a welcome gulp. "Not with the right girl."

16

On our way back to the van, we both heaved sighs of relief. "At least she won't be staying in her bedroom until tomorrow night," I said.

"That gives us a day to plan a possible plan of attack—or defense." She looked worried. "Do we even know which it's going to be?"

"I think I've got a leg up on that," I said, as I let her into the passenger side.

Self-consciously, she pulled the skirt portion down again as she swiveled into place. "That's not another excuse for you to take a gander at my gams again, is it?"

"Did you borrow those terms from some James Cagney or Edward G. Robinson movie?" I chuckled

"Can I help it if I love old mysteries?"

"As if you needed any more endearing qualities."

"And that doesn't get you off the hook from staring at

my legs!"

"Just making sure you're healing properly."

"Sure you are!" she smiled. "But it sounds like you're keeping a secret from your secretary again."

"Just a surprise—for where we'll be 'dining' tonight."

"Oh, Nicky! Not one that will let me down again?"

I went around to my side and started the engine. "It's closer to our homes. But I was hoping, if you aren't too tired, we could combine our dining out with a little—" I raised both eyebrows. "—reconnoitering?"

She tittered. "You make it sound almost naughty."

"I do? I didn't mean to. What I meant was whether you'd mind making this a working dinner, scanning through those diary pages you photographed. We might find something we can put to use in planning how we can deal with this."

She tried to stop from yawning but failed, covering it at least with a small pat of her hand. "Sorry, Nicky. That glass of wine made me sleepy. I hope I'm up to it."

The truth was, and I couldn't tell her this, not after we'd spent so much time together already, I didn't feel right about her leaving me tonight. "The more we know, the better off we'll be."

When we pulled into the parking lot of our office, she turned towards me, her smile turning to a frown. "What are you doing, Nicky?"

"What about a late-night dinner at the Grinder, just the two of us?"

"It's going on nine already." She sounded disappointed.

"Is it even open?"

"It's Friday," I said, "and open until ten."

She picked at unseen lint on the hem. "I guess at least it's not fast food or pizza again." Not exactly a rousing endorsement.

"Will another libation make it more appealing?" I used a term that harkened back to an offering to the gods—or goddesses, hoping that might soften the blow somewhat.

She made a half-hearted attempt at humor. "If it doesn't conk me out altogether."

"The menu here is really pretty varied for such a small place," I said, grasping at straws. I was desperate for her not to give up on me, though I was afraid I'd already lost her. "Cher might still be there on swing since tips are better at night on the weekends."

"You think making this a working dinner like our working lunches here will make it less of a date? Is that it?"

"Friday's fish night," I prodded. "And at least it's not the office."

She sighed heavily again. "Our satellite office, though, for a 'date.'"

"We won't spend long on the diary, I promise."

She eyed me askance but didn't say anything. Had I won—or lost in winning?

When we entered the restaurant, the homey aroma of fries and burgers overwhelmed us like a comforting wave. I pointed at a booth near the cash register counter and the window with its kitchen order wheel. "We should sit side by side to make it easier to read your phone's screen."

"That would be nice." Was she weakening? She swept a hand under the skirt of her dress unnecessarily since it was so snug anyway, then slid in first as I sidled so close we touched.

Cher was indeed on duty and quick to join us. "Well," she said, snapping her gum, eyes hollow with Friday fatigue but brightening at the sight of Randi in her bright pink dress. "Aren't you the pretty one tonight? The tail end of a hot date?"

"Not exactly the end," Randi smiled, eyes darting at me.

"The footnote to a long work day," I tried to clarify.

Cher wiggled the pencil in her hand over the order pad. "Only coffee and dessert then?" she grinned.

"The whole enchilada this time," I said.

"Really, Nicky?" Cher said. "The enchiladas really are especially good here, you know!"

"Uh, not literally. I meant the menus. We're ordering dinner tonight."

"Oh—wonderful!" She brought the menus over right away from a splined wooden holder at the side of the cash register.

"Great clam chowder today on special, too," she boasted.

"That sounds like a winner," I said.

She pointed to the paper flyer stuck into the tops of the menus. "And fish and chips are featured for two dollars off."

"A glass of wine to top off what we had earlier?" I suggested. Randi gave a hesitant nod.

"Chardonnay?" said Cher.

"We had red before," Randi mentioned. "Can we change midstream?"

"It's been hot today," I said. "Let's have the chilled Chardonnay. Goes better with fish anyway. Is that okay?"

"You got it," chirped Cher and disappeared behind the bar.

Randi strained a side look at me. "Maybe some of her energy will spill over onto me."

"I'm sure she's pumped more by the fact that there's only a couple more hours to go."

Randi sighed once more. "Are we ever going to have a normal nine-to-five workday?"

"We'll have more breathing space," I tried to assure her, "when we close this case."

She seemed even more despondent. "With a happy ending?"

I shrugged. "Maybe with the help of her diary?"

"It's the writings of a girl, not the woman who hired us to throw us off her little scheme."

"You'll feel better after you get something hot in you besides those tapas. You had only a salad for lunch, remember."

"Cold Chardonnay," said Randi with a wan smile, "and a hot meal? You want me cold—or hot?"

"Don't together they sort of cancel each other out?"

She did manage a weak smile finally. "A strange kind of togetherness."

The wine appeared in frosted goblets. I grabbed the bowl-shaped top amply full. "Saved by the bell?"

We clinked and drank. "Mmm," she said. "It does hit the spot." She turned the pages of the menu and pointed to one of the items. "Look, Nicky. They've got coconut shrimp!"

"That's only an appetizer. They've got a fried shrimp dinner or sautéed shrimp in butter with rice or potato plus a choice of salad or soup. Doesn't that sound more balanced?"

She closed the menu. "You order for me then. They all sound good. What about you?"

"I'm easy, remember?" I said. "A cup of that clam chowder and a small crab Caesar."

"Isn't that what you usually order when you go out?"

I tried to protest. "I had a blackened salmon Caesar at Stanford's and a seafood chowder."

She clucked. "Doesn't sound much different to me."

"Well, maybe I don't like variety."

"I guess I'll have to be your variety then."

"Sounds good to me!" I smiled. Maybe I'd finally won her over, if a bit grudgingly.

When Cher came back about ten minutes later after we were more than halfway through our glasses and had perused some of the diary pages, I ordered the fried shrimp and rice pilaf for her, assuring Randi we'd try the coconut shrimp as an hors d'oeuvre sometime after work later. "Something to look forward to," she conceded softly. The wine that had initially brightened her face now seemed to have turned her melancholy. That wasn't like her.

"Good choices!" said Cher with another toothy smile.

"That's my girl," I laughed as she left us alone again.

"You're not helping matters any, Nicky. Remember,

she's got kind of a crush on you."

"I can't help what she reads into things that aren't there," I said with a half-shrug.

"Hard not to." She tapped at the phone's screen. "These entries aren't like reading a person—in person. I'm not sure they're helping much."

Cher jounced back into our lives with our entrees before we had a chance to go much further. I could smell the bacon bits in the steaming clam chowder. She had brought me a biscuit without my asking because she knew I preferred that over oyster crackers.

"You can carry all that without spilling a drop?" I said.

"It took a while to get the hang of it," she answered. "But some days I do wish I had more arms—you know like that Indian goddess?"

"Shiva? Kali?" I posed.

"Lakshmi?" Randi murmured since that was our goddess of the day now.

"Whatever," Cher said.

"They all boast at least four arms," I granted. "Maybe ancient Hindu women felt the same as modern ones, looking at gods for models of what they would have liked in real life."

"Interesting," Cher chawed on her gum, suggesting she didn't really think so. Randi, though, confirmed that as a likely supposition by cocking her head and giving a thin smile.

Cher looked back behind the cashier's counter at the coffee maker. "You'll probably be wanting coffee after? I'll make a special pot just for you guys. The other's way too old. Caffeine okay—or is it too late for that?"

"Is that okay with you?" I asked Randi who agreed with some hesitation.

Cher's blue-green eyes widened. "I got ya there!"

"Am I that bad when I'm so chirpy myself?" she said. Something else was bothering her.

"She means well," I replied, "and so do you. It's more helpful than you realize."

We ate heartily at first, the phone lapsing into sleep mode. I didn't want to push her any more. She'd seemed disheartened by what we'd read so far. So was I.

Cher brought us the full carafe of coffee later with cups in saucers and a surprise.

"Uh," I said, "I don't know if we have enough room for pie, Cher."

"Take it home in a box if you like. It's on the house. Last piece of fresh blueberry pie. It's your favorite, isn't it?"

I nodded, surprised she remembered from the one I'd ordered once before. She'd even dropped a dollop of whipped cream on top. "How considerate."

She poured the coffee out for us. "Only the best for our best, honey," beamed Cher. Then she directed this at Randi. "You got a great boss here, girl." She made a double clicking noise out the side of her lips like she was spurring on a horse, winking. Then she skipped back to the counter where she'd been reading a tabloid when we entered the restaurant.

"She's going to burst a button if she's any springier!" Randi sniffed.

"It's a slow night," I smiled. "A little extra sugar and spice doesn't hurt."

"That's what I love about you, Nicky," she said, sipping at the coffee. "For being in this business, and an ex-cop at that, you can be so generous about people."

I sat back. "Have we suddenly traded places?"

She held the phone a moment before slipping it back in her purse. "I think this diamond is just the tip of the iceberg for Mena, and I feel like we're about to sideswipe it like the Titanic."

I'd already developed the same sinking feeling, and we hadn't even finished reading all the pages she'd recorded.

Cher reluctantly saw us out as I paid, slipping the tip into her apron pocket before she flipped the sign on the windowed door from "Open" to "Closed," this time with a more wrinkled wink at us, as if she'd at last timed out.

Randi hung onto my arm more heavily, as if I'd hooked too big a fish. Her voice crackled like cellophane. "Just what kind of mess did we get ourselves into here, Nicky?"

"More importantly," I added, nonplussed at her melancholy, "how are we going to get *out*?"

17

"'I want to marry someone just like Daddy,'" I repeated aloud.

Those words were scrawled in large looping letters throughout the pages we'd skimmed. We were back in the office getting ready to go our separate ways to get some rest, if that were even possible now, at least for me.

"Hardly unusual sentiments," said Randi, fingers combing through her hair as she raised her head, neck making a quiet cracking sound. "I didn't have my dad long enough since I was so young when he died. But who knows? Maybe I'd have written the same thing."

"Freud himself had a doting daughter as if he needed any more validation for the Elektra complex."

"But for Mena to fixate so long," Randi added. Mena was only ten years or so older. But maybe that was a good sign, that she allied herself more with me and the agency than with our troubled client.

I reacted simply with, "It doesn't sound like he encouraged that kind of worship either. He had to be too busy getting the baking business successful enough for them to retire so early."

"We don't really know the story from Mena's point of view, diary or not."

"All Wade ever let on," I said, "was that they were disappointed how she's turned out, maybe because of her choice for a husband. Not unusual either. Still, they gave them fifty thousand dollars."

Randy fingered the seam at her neckline now. "The only reason I can think of for her sneaking the diamond into her room is that if they willed it to a museum, she wouldn't get as much of an inheritance."

"She'd get plenty anyway—unless they've disinherited her," I said.

"If the insurance company paid up, wouldn't she get that if she's still the sole heir?"

"We might be presuming too much," I said. "We've been so focused on Wade and Addy being the victims here. What if they've brought this whole thing down on their heads themselves, and the fifty grand is a consolation prize for Mena to salve their conscience?" Most people were their own worst enemy. Most? Almost all, including yours truly. But maybe Randi suspected as much already without my saying it aloud.

Maybe she'd partially caught my drift. "Didn't you tell me he said it was a lot simpler to will the whole kit and kaboodle to a museum?"

"Something caused this rift," I said. "If she's loved her father so much, why would she hit him where it hurts the worst like this?"

"Don't they say sometimes love and hate are two sides of the same coin? That's something I've never understood."

"If it didn't have some truth to it, sweetie," I said, "they'd never need anybody like us."

"With the diamond in hand, though," Randi added, "Mena can negotiate for whatever she wants on the side."

"But," I said, "for only a few thousand bucks? Risking insurance fraud—and prison—for petty change with a 'bauble' worth millions?"

"You said it's too famous to fence," she said. "A bird in the hand, like they say."

"You're full of clichés all of a sudden."

"Didn't you say clichés are clichés for a reason? Because—" She smirked now. "—they hit the nail on the head?"

"Touché!" I laughed as I spun my desk chair around and returned to her side since she was still standing. "Regardless, we have to return the diamond to its fold."

Randi slung the strap of her purse over a shoulder, looking like she'd just swung the whole world onto her, but making a big show of trying to leave. "Either that, or call in the guys in white coats."

"She's still our client, sweetie. The real question is how much should we tell Wade, when he might not be telling us everything either."

"Why is it, Nicky, these mysteries end up with solutions we have to keep secret from so many, including the law? Isn't that just as illegal?"

"We have our clients' best interests at heart?" But that

rationalization paled, too, now.

She clasped a hand on my shoulder a moment. "We have to stand together on this and do what's right somehow. Whatever you do, I do, too."

"And together—what?" I offered lamely. "We're—'do-do'?"

"Oh, Nicky! Be serious!" She had tears in her eyes.

I held her hand now so her fingers relaxed enough to interweave with mine. "Maybe we should have stolen the diamond from *Mena* when we had the chance—and put the kibosh on the whole thing."

"Then whoever tried to attack Ava, and got me instead, or the ones who tried to nab the diamond on their own, would try to get Mena instead."

But I drew the obvious conclusion I'd already entertained. "Or *us*!"

Her lips curled as the tears finally fell. "I'm—so *scared*, Nicky!"

I pulled her head into my chest as she wept more freely, an arm about her despite that unwieldy bag of hers that she finally let drop to the floor. The warmth of her tears melted into me, the wetness seeping through my turtleneck and T-shirt. It felt good.

To comfort her and maybe myself, I gently kissed the top of her head, luxuriating in the briny smell of her tears, the citrusy fragrance of her hair, the caramel scent rising up from her face.

Then she followed her outburst with something that sent an electric ripple up my spine that made me dizzy. "I don't want you to leave me alone tonight!"

18

That posed another problem now. How to please Randi and make her feel comfortable with a temporary compromise? "Why not come home with me tonight? You can have the bedroom. I've got a hide-a-bed in the front room for me."

"A sofa again, after you spent last night on one?"

"It converts to a queen-sized bed with a thick enough mattress. So don't worry about me. It's surprisingly comfortable." Then I added, "I'm not sure you'd be as safe at your place anyway, what with all the feathers we've ruffled lately." That was a polite way of telling her I didn't think her apartment was really in a very safe part of town without saying it outright. Sadly, a lot of pussyfooting going around lately, on everybody's part.

"I've got clothes here in the office I can change into tomorrow," she said, sniffling so that I offered her my handkerchief again, rather than her digging in her purse for those tiny packages of Kleenex she used for blotting her lipstick.

That handkerchief was getting a real workout lately. “And this time when we stopped by my apartment, I did put some extra underwear in my purse.”

“What a relief!” I smiled faintly. “You’ve sort of moved in here anyway.”

“Don’t worry,” she said with an incipient smile. “‘Here’ isn’t your home.” She wiped her nose and eyes, face streaked with mascara though she seemed self-conscious about the dark stains on the white linen. I shrugged it off the way a gentleman’s supposed to, even if it might not be the way of the day anymore. Then again I was used to being a stranger in a strange land.

“Almost,” I smiled, not wanting to let her go though I’d had to.

“I’d feel better about this case if we spent the next couple of nights together until it’s over.”

“So would *I*.” She didn’t need me to elaborate.

“By ‘together,’” she clarified, “I mean together ‘apart,’ you know.”

It didn’t sound like she *did* know. Neither did I. But I still said, “I do.”

We did at least as I promised, she taking her yellow Malibu to my place. I gave her one of my pale blue pajama tops since she obviously hadn’t brought sleepwear to the office closet.

“No bottoms?” she said.

“I don’t know what I did with them.” That was mostly true. I’d lost track since I stopped wearing them with Angie, the tops long enough but allowing me more freedom since I was a restless sleeper at best.

She looked at me, both eyebrows raised. Nonetheless, she tried one on, announcing from behind the half-closed door that the sleeves were too long. "But I guess it covers enough to keep me decent because I'm shorter."

I took her at her word but didn't see for myself until I woke her from a very deep sleep the next morning and she came out for the coffee I'd made that she could smell, parading in it before me while also demurely tugging down that hem, too, which was far shorter than her dresses. "Very stylish, huh," she said, fanning it out slightly before climbing up onto one of the bar stools in the kitchen island where I'd been scanning the morning paper, mostly the same sentences over and over again. Not much in this slim excuse for a newspaper anyway since *The Oregonian* had gone digital and changed its part-time print version to a tabloid format.

"It serves the purpose," I grinned, "but your dresses do more for you."

"Wait until you see what I've got in store for Addy's homecoming—and tomorrow's showdown."

"I can hardly wait." She'd made every day into a new debut I looked forward to.

"And I've decided how I can repay you for what you did for me last night."

"Oh?" I said uncertainly, not sure what she had in mind. After all, hadn't she done what I'd wanted all along after I'd already compromised our "dinner date" last night with homework?

"Once we find out what Mena's plans are for her mystery rendezvous tomorrow, I want to treat you tonight to something I've been planning for when the time was right."

"Aren't you going to tell me?"

"Not yet," she demurred. "I don't want you to be disappointed. Better to keep it a mystery."

"As if we don't have enough already?"

"This one at least will have a happy ending." She slipped down off the stool, the hem catching on the vinyl seat enough to give me a fleeting glimpse of her "Saturday" panties and a wink she cast over her shoulder. Did she know that had come across as a double entendre? I couldn't be sure anymore.

An hour or so later, when I'd gotten dressed and was making her some of my puffy whole grain pancakes with turkey bacon ("real crisp" the way she liked it), she came out, her face flushed and shiny from obviously just having taken another shower. She swirled about in what she explained was a black-and-white Entourage dress with short rucked sleeves, a white ruffled side slit over the leg that didn't expose her garter holster and an asymmetrical hem trimmed with the same frills.

"It looks like a Chiquita dress that Carmen Miranda might have worn in her heyday."

She tilted her head quizzically at me until finally brightening again. "You mean that Brazilian singer from the Forties with those big fruity headdresses?"

I gave a throaty life. "Now I'm convinced you're a fifty-year-old hiding inside the lovely body of a twenty-something!"

She grinned as she fluttered the skirt, raising it discreetly. "And see? Not as many bandages now."

"A sight for my very sore eyes," I said hoping they didn't

look as bloodshot as they felt.

"Mmm," she said. "Pancakes and bacon?"

I called on Cher's catchphrase. "Only the best for my guest."

She peered at the platter, sniffing, as I was about to scoop out the last batch. "These pancakes look sinfully delicious."

"Happy to tempt you then," I smiled and nodded for her to sit down at the place setting where I'd positioned a platter of turkey bacon, indicating the plastic container full of low-fat syrup I'd just re-heated in the microwave.

"Wicked," she said, "but in a good way."

Then I explained the plan I'd set in motion since we knew Mena would be staying overnight in her old bedroom to retrieve the diamond for whatever deal she meant to deliver on Sunday morning.

"An old-fangled bug?" she said.

"Whether she uses a cell phone or the landline, we'll overhear."

"That's assuming she hasn't already made arrangements."

"If that's true, then we'll tail her to the rendezvous point."

Randi lowered her eyes. "The people she's slighted aren't about to take this lying down."

"Either way," I said, patting at my holster, "we'll be ready to save what we have to."

"Mena?"

"Ultimately," I said, "the diamond, not to mention Wade and Addy."

"And," she intoned, "let's hope us, too."

19

When we arrived at the Huntingtons shortly after noon, Wade and Mena were having a late brunch on the patio outside the breakfast nook, Maria already fussing at the stove making preparations for what we presumed to be dinner later on. She needed another hobby! Peter hadn't brought Addy home from the hospital yet, though the doctor had led everyone to believe she'd be released "mid-day."

"You know doctors," clucked Wade. "The patients are impatient to get home but doctors sign the release forms in their own sweet time." Peter had called to say only that the release wouldn't happen until sometime "after two or so."

We looked at Mena carefully. She seemed perturbed, too, but we suspected it was because her own plans might still be up in the air. We stayed passing the time somewhat awkwardly with them outside on the deck until Addy showed up finally after three, slouching, clearly exhausted though ably assisted by Peter's strong arms.

"You must stay for afternoon tea," Addy offered hoarsely with a glance Maria's way who nodded back an affirmation that she would take care of it.

"You need your rest for tomorrow," I said.

"He's right, dear," Wade agreed, approaching her side but Addy waving him off.

"I need to get on in the house on my own again," she insisted.

Wade looked better rested today. Still, I didn't think tea was his drink of choice even this early in the afternoon by the way he screwed up his face without Addy noticing, shrugging privately at me. But we accepted her gesture to please her, this British tea party hosted back on the patio during another gorgeous summery afternoon. The "crumpets" Wade joked about were freshly baked cheesy flax and quinoa biscuits courtesy of Maria.

Surprisingly, the tea seemed to revitalize Addy, or maybe it was just being home again at long last, though her eyes began to droop before the hour was up. "Maybe a little nap before dinner would be nice," she finally conceded. We could smell the yeasty fragrance of fresh bread dough rising as Maria flurried about the full house again, obviously delighted to have the whole family together again. When we asked Mena about her husband, she said he was busy with his hobbies. "He loves working on his projects in the garage on the weekends," she explained. "I doubt he'll join us tonight." We figured it was more complicated than that.

In her renewed buoyancy, Maria again asked us to stay

for dinner.

"Thanks, Maria," Randi apologized, "but I've got plans of my own for Nicky."

When we bid everyone goodbye around half past four, Mena smiled with what looked like relief, Addy not yet up from her nap but Wade already headed for the liquor cabinet. He reminded us of the time and place for the ceremony—one o'clock at the Lutheran church near the old Ashborough high school. We told him we'd try to make it but warned that we had some duties with higher priorities to take care of first. That resulted in a wary side glance from Mena.

On our way back to the van, Randi said, "Mena knows we know more than we're letting on."

"It'll keep that little muliebral Machiavelli guessing," I said.

"Whatever *that* means!" she laughed with a smirk. "The girl's pretty witchy."

"That's what I said," I smiled back. "We just have to be witchier."

Randi cocked her head at my obliqueness. "Let's start with me trying to be-witch you tonight," she quipped.

I groaned. "I think you just got me in the heart with your pun gun."

She giggled. "Sorry! But there's more fun to come."

"I was afraid of that. So what's on tonight's call board?"

"A little calm," she said, "before tomorrow's storm."

"So where are we going exactly?"

She clapped her hands. "Tonight you're having dinner

with me at my place!"

I was happy to see her so energized but worried, too. "Even with all we're about to face?"

"*Because* of that," she said. "We can monitor Mena's cloak-and-dagger shenanigans from my place just as well as anywhere, and more comfortably than the office or your van. You know what they say about how best to prepare for a big test."

"Eat well and get a good night's rest?" I ventured.

"Tonight you'll be *my* guest. Tit for tat, right?"

"Uh—"

"I want to prove to you I'm no slouch in the kitchen so we don't have to go out all the time." She fluttered her eyelids down. "It'll be safer staying together again before whatever tomorrow brings."

"That sounds really nice, sweetie," I granted. "But we can't settle on a strategy until we find out what her plans are."

"That doesn't mean we can't enjoy the evening while we wait."

Although I was flattered she wanted to reciprocate this way, I still felt my home was more defensible than her apartment. She acted oblivious to the complex being located in a questionable part of town where the city's gentrification efforts in the Seventies had degenerated with the influx of migrants picking that area to locate during the double-digit mortgage rates of the Eighties glutted rental units and crime rates there began to soar. The intruders Thursday night knew we'd defended the manor where they somehow found out Mena had stashed the diamond. What if they now thought *we'd* taken it for safekeeping—and found out where we lived? Not hard to do in the world where Google had become Big Brother. They may not have been professional thieves but with backgrounds in the sciences, they certainly weren't stupid either.

I didn't want to share these misgivings with Randi when she seemed so well-meaning. For the time being, I found refuge in humor. "I guess the real boss here has spoken."

"Hey," Randi said, elbowing me. "I'm just being nice."

I flinched, acting like she'd done more harm than she had. "So *this* is what 'sidekick' really means?"

She laughed as we entered the thick of Saturday evening traffic backing up on Tenth Avenue as it curved into Tualatin Valley Highway before we could turn off into her apartment complex. Next door stood an L-shaped strip mall anchored by an all-you-can-eat Izzy's restaurant directly opposite Shute Park's towering fir trees and the site of the Ashborough city library's annex, both of which contributed to the bottleneck. "The noise of the traffic here and that Southern Pacific train line along the highway doesn't bother you?"

"The rent's cheap," she contended. Of course that was also the reason so many indigents had chosen the region.

The parking lot itself offered no relief with its din of noisy car mufflers as some vehicles revved up to depart while I searched for a safe place close to her unit. I echoed Quasimodo's plea. "*Sanctuary, sanctuary!*"

At least she laughed at that without me explaining it.

"It's worse Friday and Saturdays," she said. "But you know me. I can sleep through thunderstorms and earthquakes."

I'd seen that firsthand, a talent I longed someday to emulate. "Maybe I'd better raise your salary so you can afford something better." I'd been considering that anyway, since this case might pay off better than our first one. Her improvised striptease Thursday just made her support that much sweeter.

She hesitated. "It's still a posh townhouse for the money."

"Sometimes you get more than what you pay for, not always for the better."

"Fortune cookie wisdom again?"

I shrugged but with a smile.

"You want me to move closer to the office?"

"And to me," I said, then added hastily so she wouldn't misunderstand, "where it's safer."

She arched an eyebrow. "I wouldn't want you to be ashamed of me, since we're hobnobbing with Ashborough's finest now."

"A classy dame like you? Never!"

"Oh, Nicky. Why'd you have go ruin it with that kind of talk!"

"I love old detective stories, too!"

That helped her laugh it off.

As I helped her out to show up anyone there, although no one noticed, her stomach made a noise like a kitten purring. She slapped a hand over her abdomen. "Darn this body of mine!"

"I'm not complaining," I chuckled. "But I guess we *did* miss lunch again. Tea and crumpets this afternoon didn't compensate enough?"

"I'll fix something to carry us through till dinner. Maybe cheese puffs?"

"You never cease to amaze."

"All part of the package." She returned a small, complacent smile while unlocking her front door, starting to let me in. I insisted she lead the way, though, because I was carrying in the receiver under one arm. Luckily, I had a hand at the small of her back just as she tripped over the metal threshold and somehow steadied her without dropping the machine.

She cast an embarrassed glance over her shoulder. "Nice save. Believe me, Nicky, that's not a preview of what's to come. I am *not* a klutz!"

I smiled. "At least you know I've always got your back."

"Don't forget my front," she teased. "One kind of goes with the other."

I had to bite my tongue at that one since it was a very nice front, settling for, "I'm glad you reminded me."

I laid the receiver down on the built-in desk, where a wireless blue phone sat upright in its cradle, and plugged it in, turning the dial down to minimize the static.

"I've got something for you to do that's right up your alley while I mix the batter for the appetizer," she said slyly.

I cocked my head now at her uncertainly. "Oh?"

She pulled a bottle of Chardonnay off the door of the refrigerator, then handed it to me by its neck with a steel instrument that looked like something from Torquemada's Spanish Inquisition. "I dub thee our official cork puller!"

I raised both eyebrows, unable to arch just one like her. "What? No electric one?"

She poked my chest with a finger. "You have to work for your supper here, buster. But you won't be slumming by any means." She presented me with two long-stemmed goblets. As she wrapped herself in a frilly white apron trimmed with pink ruffles, I performed my duty with pretended solemnity and poured.

"To us being better together while armed," I said, clicking the tips of the glasses.

"Then let's do this properly for good luck," she insisted. We linked arms in a pretzel toast that threatened to make us spill, though we quickly rebalanced the glasses without spilling.

"You can take that off now," she said of my shoulder holster. "I won't bite—much anyway."

The persistent noise from the parking lot made me hesitate a moment before I doffed my jacket and holster. It was too warm inside anyway.

Randi then drew out chicken breasts from the freezer atop the refrigerator that she defrosted in a bowl of warm water in the porcelain sink. In a cut-glass bowl she emptied a package of Romaine lettuce and took out a jar of light Cardini Caesar salad dressing. "How do chicken croquettes and cheese drop biscuits sound with your favorite salad?"

"Plying me with wine would have been enough," I joked. "Like you, I'm easy, remember?"

"Hmm," she hummed, an eyebrow arched before taking out a tenderizing hammer.

"Your tools of the trade do look like arms of another kind," I joked.

"I want to make sure the breasts are so tender they'll melt in your mouth," she grinned, "and still be crunchy outside, or they wouldn't be 'croquettes.'"

"Sort of like my favorite candy," I said.

"Which is?"

"Mountain Bar, Brigittine Monastery's dark truffles, and dark chocolate sea foam."

"What the heck is that last one?"

"I'll have to introduce you to some from the Candy Basket downtown."

"I don't know, Nicky. Hard to beat white chocolate covered pretzels!"

We each took a sip of the wine as she folded in the batter for the cheese puffs. But I couldn't help glaring out at the front window where she had the blinds tilted down, the shadows of the towering Douglas firs of Shute Park lengthening this far already as the sun dipped behind. "Don't they ever settle down?"

"The natives do seem overly restless tonight," she granted. "It'll get better after the kids leave on their dates."

I went to the window to peer through the slats at the side of the flimsy drapery when the receiver let out a squawk. "Turn up the volume," I said to her. Quickly she did.

Then we heard Mena's voice more distinctly. "She's talking to someone in her bedroom!" Randi whispered eagerly.

I pricked up my ears trying despite the squealing tires outside. The words warbled, the reception not the best until we finally made out, "You know the new Ron Tonkin Athletic Field north of town near Sunset Highway?"

She sounded far away, apparently on her cell phone rather than the landline where we'd hidden the bug. "You got what I asked for? . . . Good. Remember, it's only on loan. . . Tomorrow morning half past eight then?"

The reception hissed like a serpent.

"Sounds like one of those old crystal radios," whispered Randi.

"You get what you pay for," I smirked, since she knew these were hand-me-downs.

Randi took a longer swallow from her wine glass. "It's set then," she sighed. "I was hoping we wouldn't have to wake up so early."

I cocked my head at her with the way she said that, but the racket outside distracted me even as I replied with a shake of my head. "In a crummy ballfield yet."

"But it'll all be over soon, Nicky."

"There is that."

Randi checked the window in the built-in oven. "The cheese puffs won't take long."

I went back to the window but couldn't see much through the blinds, the dappled sunlight making it harder. In the rippling shadows, though, I thought I saw sequential turning lights flash as a car swerved right out onto Tenth. "Mind if I check the van a second? It's been crazy out there." I could have sworn I heard the distinct sound of motorcycles circling right outside her door. I'd parked in an empty slot at the end of a row so only one side of the van could be dinged even though the van came with bump guards.

"Just don't be gone long, okay?"

I had to put my mind at ease that the van hadn't been sideswiped or keyed during all that pandemonium. After stepping outside, I could smell the lingering stench of the exhausts, but also a hint of the dusty heat, too, grateful at least some of the noise had diminished, the lot emptier. Then it caught my eye, the yellow slip tucked into the base of the window on the driver's side. I took it off, read it and clucked, stuffing it into my jean pocket, not sure I should tell Randi.

When I rejoined her inside, the unit was redolent with the homey fragrance of baked cheese. She had taken out the chicken breasts beating them with the stippled square head of the metal mallet.

"Taking out your frustrations?" I said with a crooked smile.

"Want to try your hand at it?" she said. "Cooking can be really therapeutic." Of course I'd already learned that trying to recreate some of the favorite meals I'd once shared.

"You look like you're doing fine on your own." Randi was rolling up the flattened pieces and dipping them in a bowl with egg and milk before coating them in another dish with bread crumbs that smelled of Italian seasoning and parmesan.

"I could use a short slurp though," she said, hands too

sticky to hoist the glass, looking for me to help. "Got to lubricate the cook enough to cook!"

"Hmm," I smirked. But I obliged her by holding the glass to her lips, tilting it carefully. "I guess this is what's called 'nursing' your drink?" That made her snuffle out a badly repressed laugh, some wine trickling to the front of her apron.

"At least some went down my throat!" she coughed.

"And you didn't snort any out your nose," I added.

"Nicky!"

"Sorry." I wiped some off her chin with my ever-handy handkerchief.

She finished preparing the tray of croquettes and placed it in the oven, still hot from the cheese puffs, then washed off her hands and sat back up at the breakfast bar with me to sip more from the glass on her own as she sampled the hors d'oeuvres urging me to take one which I did.

"The biscuits and potatoes won't take long with my short cuts," she said, indicating the packages on the counter with Bisquick and the Idahoan instant red potato mix. "I'm giving away the trade secrets to my 'scratch' recipes."

"Every day I learn something more about you."

"Me, too, you," she smiled back.

"But I don't know much about your past."

"Because," she smirked, "I don't have much of one yet."

"You got me there," I said.

"You already know my dad died when I was just a teenager. An accident at Tektronix when he was crushed by a pile of pipes that rolled over him. Mom got a settlement that helped her finish raising us, but you never get over something like that. Not news to you. Something you couldn't stop that you wanted to."

I took another sip, noting her use of the word "us." "But a looker like you—no boyfriend yet?"

"The one in college was enough to last me a while," she said gazing into my eyes. "But like you keep saying, the story's still being written."

"Even for this old codger."

"You're not that old, Nicky. Not to me."

I glanced over at the Caesar salad on the nearby kitchen counter and gave into temptation, plucking out a couple leaves of Romaine to munch.

She pretended to chasten me with the tap of a finger on my hand. "Hey! Wait till we sit down at the table like civilized people."

"Delicious," I said anyway. She'd already dressed and sprinkled it with parmesan.

"No anchovies, though," she said.

"Tastes great as it is." I thought for sure I could detect a hint of anchovies, though. Cardini, the originator, had featured them in his first makeshift recipe and she was using dressing with his name on it, so I was pretty sure it must include at least anchovy paste. But if she didn't think it was there, I wasn't about to call that to her attention. Sometimes self-deception could be a plus.

She turned up the volume to the portable CD player crammed onto the desk next to the receiver. Through its tinny speakers streamed romantic piano music, songs from famous films. I recognized “My Own True Love” from “Gone with the Wind” to which she swayed slightly, the back of her dress hypnotic like a rippling curtain.

The homey warmth from the nearby oven with the inner warmth from the wine was making me feel the wine. Randi acted like she was, too.

“It’s pleasant inside right now,” I said, “but you’ll probably have to turn the air-conditioning up if you’re going to get any sleep in your bedroom upstairs.”

“The place doesn’t have any. Not like your house.”

“Oh, Randi,” I said. “You’ll be sweltering up there.” It had risen into the high eighties outside again.

“I’m used to it. I don’t wear much to bed anyway. You already know that. Is it too warm for you right now?”

Well, in a way next to her it was. “It’s fine,” I lied.

“I—” She hesitated. “I was kind of hoping you might stay there on the sofa tonight with me. You made me feel stronger when we spent the night together.”

I leveled my eyes on her.

“The sofa is fairly comfortable, I think,” she said. “Unless you’d rather sleep in your own bed tonight. I hogged it before.”

“Let’s play it by ear,” I said. That troubling post-it note and the sounds outside made me hesitate, but I was thinking along the same lines already.

“Dinner will be ready in twenty minutes or so, enough for us to have another glass of wine if you want.”

I was almost done with mine before she refilled us. “Could I help set the table?”

"I'll get the plates and silverware," she said, "but you can light the candle."

The dinette on the other side of the U-shaped kitchen featured a small square table she had covered with a white lace-trimmed crocheted tablecloth. A red candle sat in its candlestick at the center, complete with bobeche. She got the Melmac dishes down from the cabinet though it was a reach for her that hiked up her skirt slightly, then gave me the silverware as she pointed to the lighter on the table.

I took the gold Colibri Wellington flint lighter out of my pocket, the note crinkling there as I did. "I've got my own, remember."

"But you don't smoke."

"It's another keepsake my father kept with him like the pocket knife, even though he never smoked either. Just a boy scout at heart, I guess." I lit the candle, then started to arrange the silverware, trying to remember what Mom had taught me about proper placement.

Quietly she replaced the butter knife on the right side facing in next to the spoon rather than on the left next to the fork. "Etiquette," she said, "is actually pretty practical, you know."

"Sorry," I shrugged awkwardly.

"You came close, Nicky. An A- for 'attempt'?" She removed the croquettes from the oven using a silver tong to put them into a serving bowl along with the salad before placing the biscuits and potatoes on the table.

"Smells wonderful," I said as I bent to sit down.

She hesitated a moment. "What's that paper sticking out

of your pocket?"

I blanched, not realizing the tip now showed. "It's nothing really."

"We're partners, Nicky. We can't keep secrets from each other for long."

I took another gulp of wine. "You don't miss a thing, do you."

"Isn't that part of what you're training me to do?"

"I—didn't want to worry you."

"In case you haven't noticed, I'm a big girl, Nicky. What is it?"

"Someone stuck it on the window of the van," I finally admitted. "Maybe just kids putting us on."

"Let me see."

I relented with a heavy sigh and slid it over to her so she could read what had been scrawled across in all-caps with what looked like a black Sharpie:

"*STAY OUT OF THIS!*"

20

She motioned me to sit down as she did now, the apron still on. “We’re in this together, Nicky, remember.”

I paused. “The players can’t know yet what we’re going to do. We didn’t ourselves until a short while ago.”

“Someone’s trying to scare us,” she said, “and doing a pretty good job of it.”

“They’re just playing mind games,” I told her. “They hadn’t slashed the tires or anything. That’s why I thought at first it might be just kids. But now you know why I hesitated when you suggested I stay with you again tonight. You might not be safe alone.”

“I wanted you to but was afraid to ask,” she finally admitted. “Maybe this nice meal will help us sleep better afterwards.” She didn’t sound convinced.

I started to eat, seeing what she meant about the croquettes’ crunchiness outside and the tenderness inside.

"Delicious," I said. "But you're eating like a bird."

Her smile wavered. "Birds actually eat a lot more than people think though it looks like they're only pecking. You know me. Whatever I eat, I'll still be hungry again in no time."

I ate the helping she'd offered at first, then took two more partly to please her but also because the dish tasted so good. She worked only on her first serving.

"Then you don't mind staying with me one more night?"

Once again I hesitated. "You know it's going to be cooler down here than upstairs."

She offered another weak smile. "Is that an invitation?"

"Just—saying," I stammered.

"I'll be okay with you down here playing my guardian angel," she said. "We'll relax with some decaf coffee on the couch over there and you can tell if it's too soft for you to sleep on. I'm saving dessert for tomorrow after we see this thing through."

"I'll help clean the dishes first," I offered.

"With the dishwasher, it shouldn't take long," she said, sounding distant.

I helped stack the dishwasher as she put away the left-overs. Then she made the coffee.

"I am kind of warm already, Nicky. Is it okay if I take off some of these clothes and get into my bathrobe?"

"Be comfortable," I said. "This is your home."

"But look at you, Nicky. Your drenched under your arms. Your shirts are going to become part of your skin! I can wash your T-shirt and turtleneck, if you want."

"I'll just air them out overnight and sleep in my shorts."

She shook her head once. "You guys."

I was plenty warm all right from the meal and the cooling oven—and from her nearness.

"I'll bring down the bedclothes while you try out the sofa," she said and went upstairs while the coffee dripping supplemented the lingering aroma from the chicken and biscuits. She liked it as strong as I did.

When the Bunn coffeemaker finished, I poured her cup as well as my own and brought them both on the saucers to the coffee table in front of the sofa, sipping, still savoring the taste of the dinner, but also the company, which had made everything taste better. The wine obviously contributed to the sense of well-being despite the menace in that message.

She came down the stairs carrying the folded bedclothes in both arms and saw that I'd set up her side with two throw pillows she'd probably prop in her lap once she sat down. She set the sheets, blanket and pillow down on the rocker-recliner and turned around, cinching the belt to a pink robe with its shiny satin lapels, adjusting the seam more tightly closed at the top though not before I noticed she'd already removed her bra.

"This is just like sleepovers when we were teenagers!" she smiled, dimples prominent.

"Not exactly the same as guys staying with guys—and girls with girls," I remarked.

"Co-ed does make it more interesting, doesn't it. And the way we're doing it, me at your place last night and mine tonight, doesn't that make them 'progressive sleepovers'?"

I tilted my head. "'Progressive' how?"

"Not the way you're thinking, silly! I mean like in progressive dinners moving from house to house."

She took her place next to me, sitting as close as we had in the booth the night before. She clattered her cup back into its saucer on the coffee table after taking a sip and slithered even closer as she carefully scissored her legs up onto the couch. "See? I can do this again already."

"Don't push yourself too much," I said, realizing it was difficult turning my head towards her. "You don't want to break open any scabs." I opened my arm onto the back of the couch. She took that as welcoming her into the crook of my arm where she snuggled her head.

"Mmmm," she said shifting it deeper. "We fit just right, don't we—kind of like pieces in a puzzle?" Then she placed the flat of her left hand against the chest of my turtleneck. "I see what you mean. Even though you're sweaty, you smell nice—like leather."

"Thank you—I think." I slouched a little myself, intoxicated by her cotton candy scent.

I'm not sure how much time actually passed but before I knew it, her breathing had slowed to a soft quiet rhythm. She had fallen asleep already!

It was enchanting how easily she lapsed into such a restful sleep, her left hand slipping down my chest, confirming she was out. I sat like that for I don't know how long, enjoying her restfulness which I hoped would be infectious until I felt a needling sensation in my left arm from its having fallen asleep, too. Sadly, not the rest of me. I jostled her a little, not wanting to wake her, knowing I had to get some rest somehow. Besides, I needed to get the blood flowing back in my arm.

I knew then what I had to do. I took her in my arms like Rhett Butler and carried her up the stairs, figuring she would probably wake as I did. But she surprised me again by not doing what I expected. When I eased into her bedroom, smelling its fragrant freshness despite the blast of heat, and elbowed on the light switch, I was delighted at the brightness of the comforter's floral pattern on her double bed. The shammed pillows propped against the bookshelf headboard that matched the ruffles dangling down from the thick mattress seemed particularly feminine. I laid her down gently as she stirred while I tried to inch the covers back with my left hand still beneath her so I could cup her onto the pink sheets. I hoped she'd finally wake and take over herself, but she stayed out, only lolling her head and soughing out a slight groan as I adjusted her onto one of the pillows. I wisped strands of hair away from her eyes with a finger as I considered sliding open the anodized aluminum window behind the ribbon-tied swag curtains color-coordinated with the comforter but feared night noises would disturb her, doubting it would ever admit a breeze for lack of a vent elsewhere in the unit.

I looked down at her, seeing the seam of her robe had parted at her legs and puckered at the top with my carrying her. Should I try to free her shoulders of the robe and slip it out from under her? Or would that be unseemly now since she wore no bra? The humane thing would be to free her of the robe and try not to look while I covered her with the bedclothes—and just hope to God she didn't wake in the middle. I'd already proved I wasn't very good at *not* looking, but I could try. She'd know when she woke later. But it wouldn't be quite as embarrassing explaining my predicament in the cooler light of morning.

So I wriggled her out of her robe and swiftly swept the covers over her. Incredibly, she only moaned a little. Try as I might, I couldn't help glimpsing her perfectly rounded, firm breasts, blushing even as they burned themselves into my memory.

My God! I thought. How could I be so lucky to hire such a beautiful girl who actually enjoyed working with me?

That thought as I switched off her light and tiptoed down the stairs to make my own bed on the sofa kept me awake for hours. I stripped down to my briefs, finding a plastic clothes hanger for my turtleneck and T-shirt which I hung from the handle of her guest closet door. The blanket and sheets kept me plenty warm enough with the room still muggy but slowly cooling. Finally, sometime past midnight I did manage to fall into a restless twilight sleep, assailed by the fear of how many ways tomorrow's confrontation could go wrong—and hoping somehow they wouldn't.

21

I awoke understandably exhausted but to the welcome smell of bacon being microwaved. The whine of the machine blended with the whirring from a lingering dream about a buzz saw's blade that had broken loose like a deadly Frisbee that I had to duck to avoid. No sense scaring Randi with that or she'd think I was crazy. Strike that. She already had to know. That's what kept me in this equally crazy business. Maybe her, too.

The warmth from the covers had at least let me sleep without sweating since I wore so little. I could hear her humming to a tune from the CD player she had on while she busied herself in the kitchen wearing her bathrobe again. The song was an instrumental of "Unchained Melody" that made me think more now of "Ghost" rather than the Righteous Brothers. I slipped on my jeans which I'd draped over the sofa's arm at my feet, grabbing the T-shirt from the closet door, leaving the turtleneck for later. If the heat persisted today with the official advent of summer, I'd give up the undershirt for the season.

I sauntered into the kitchen in my stocking feet, not wanting to startle her since she was facing the drop-in stove making something in a Teflon frying pan. "So," she said without turning around, hearing me shuffle to her, "you disrobed me last night to—tuck me in?" That pause before "tuck" was particularly pregnant.

"I didn't want you to suffocate from the heat."

"The perfect gentleman?" she said finally swiveling about with lips pursed.

"Well," I blushed, "not exactly perfect."

"I was in a kind of twilight sleep, I think, half-in, half-out. I dreamt I was getting ready for a stage show and someone kept trying to sneak a peek through the curtains."

I cleared my throat. "Interesting."

"Isn't it though?" She noticed my attire. "What's with the James Dean look?"

"Isn't this proper enough?" I said.

"Very—Fifties," she said, lips pursed.

"It won't take me long to get ready to leave."

"Unlike me. We have to be out at the ballfield before the other players show up. I knew I'd need more time to gird up for action today than you would. But I wanted us to have a little something first. Scrambled eggs okay?"

"After all you served up last night?"

"Are you talking about dinner," she said, "or that glance you stole while I was unconscious?"

Softly, I repeated, "I just wanted you to be comfortable."

"I was. Were you?" But before I could respond, she turned back to the pan and scraped the eggs into two plates, then gestured for me to sit at the very short breakfast bar. "Eggs and bacon plus some leftover biscuits seemed quick and easy so we can make it there in time."

"What did you mean, 'gird up'?"

"Maybe I should have said 'girl up,'" she teased. "My version of a girl scout uniform, you might say." She poured out a generous helping for both of us before hoisting herself to the bar stool where she gestured for me to eat as she started in heartily herself, the coffee cups already filled.

She'd whipped up the eggs so they were fluffier somehow, probably doing the whites separate before combining the yolks and added more seasoning than just pieces of ham that did complement the bacon. She swallowed the last from her plate as I got up and brought them to the sink to rinse off. "I must have you trained already," she joked.

"I'm a quick learner," I rejoined, using her same line. Then she disappeared up the stairs.

I decided to wash my face and hopefully shave at least. I located a plastic razor she must have used for her legs and lathered my face with the Dove soap, missing an aftershave balm. I hadn't been prepared for overnighting elsewhere again, though I guess I'd put her through the same thing the night before, though I'd trained her already without meaning to, she's now more prepared than I was. I slipped on my turtleneck and holster before donning my jacket and stared up the stairs nervous as a beau facing an unusually treacherous prom night.

By eight she marched down the stairs in a short black wraparound mini-skirt, the surplice curving up her left leg like a crescent moon. The feathered tail of the fabric belt dangled down from the seam at the side of her drop waist that just barely exposed her navel beneath a straight-hemmed loose pink halter-top that hung free. Beneath her knees that still bore a yellowish bruise rose black leather boots with simple heels. She lifted one of her legs crossways to show me the rippled tread of the sole. "They're actually winter boots lined with rabbit fur that protect my legs better and shouldn't slip as easily either." Raising her leg sideways also parted the seam of the skirt, letting me glimpse the lace garter holster with its Kel-Tek P-11 snugged inside her left thigh this time, so she could reach the butt of the gun easily with her right hand.

"Do I live up to the 'Ready Randi' label?"

"Loaded for baring, that's for sure," I smirked.

"Armed," she said, "but cautious."

"Better than 'dangerous,' I think," I said. "But won't you be too hot in those boots?"

She fanned the short bottom of her top tantalizingly and swished her skirt. "Built-in air-conditioning." Then she plied open the slash pocket at the right side of the skirt. "And a place to squirrel away the diamond once we get it back."

"You lend a different meaning to the word 'hot,'" I said. "Let's just hope the diamond doesn't end up like a pea in a shell game there."

"And that I don't let you down again, Nicky."

"I think," I said, "you're more Don Quixote here than I am."

"Knights," she offered with devilishly twinkling eyes, "in shining amour?"

"Oh, you're priceless, sweetie!" I groaned.

"Like a diamond?"

"A diamond has a price. You don't!"

"I'm glad you think so, darling," she said with a twitch of a smile. "Now let's hope we can convince the others of that!"

22

We reached the Ron Tonkin sports field just before half-past eight, entering from 229th off Evergreen, surprised but relieved that it seemed empty, the gates unlocked. Despite its escalating population approaching one hundred thousand now, Ashborough still retained a small-town feel enough to act more trusting than many communities that had endured a similar fate even in uncertain times like this. Though they lay at the city's northernmost boundary along Sunset Highway, these grounds offered a remoteness that made an ideal rendezvous point for Mena to hand off the diamond. Because some fields also offered an uninterrupted view of the Willamette Valley in almost every direction, except where the stadiums sat, they could accommodate the archeologists' experiment with the morning sun since we'd deduced they had to be the ones she'd negotiated with on the side, though they had acted like innocents when we'd met them. Not the first time we'd been duped, or the last. The solstice occurring at 9:38 made the "borrowing" far more time-sensitive than whatever GEOS had in mind for the gem.

We parked the van on the southernmost end in the small lot near the dog park beside some plantings as we scanned the fields for any sign of movement. Nothing yet, that we could detect.

"These scientists seem to be cutting things awfully close," I said.

But Randi was looking around before she finally said with her typical form of glibness, "Ugh."

I couldn't tell at first what she'd sighted. "Anything wrong?"

She indicated the stark bow-shaped aluminum bleachers that flanked the west side of one field from the other separated by a grander, wooden one. "Those bleachers look like an Erector set gone crazy." Its slanted metal canopy looked like an afterthought resembling more the half-opened lid of a tin can.

I pointed. "The wooden grandstand that overlooks that field to the east looks like better cover."

"We're fine right here for now near the ticket booth," said Randi. A storage shed, its flap on one side closed and locked, afforded us further cover beyond the booth until we knew where the meeting would take place.

As we both scanned the deep shadows of the grandstand, though, she must have noticed what I had. Something had startled pigeons from the crooks in the rafters of the grandstand, though they were jittery creatures anyway. It wouldn't have taken much.

I knew from seeing the practice at the Hare Field stadium near where I lived now, that some dedicated runners often used the stairs for exercise. "It could be someone in the shadows sprinting up and down the steps." I hoped I was wrong. The last thing we needed were civilians muddying up this confrontation.

"Whatever scared the birds isn't moving now." But the two knots at the middle of her forehead remained.

I squinted into the shadows, holding up the flat of my hand to shade the glare caused by the rising sun glancing off all that metal, but couldn't make anything out for sure either. It would have been easy to hide, though, in a complex whose fields and structures sprawled across ninety acres.

The forecast was for another hot day, this time in the low nineties, unusual here even for the first day of summer. Randi's cell phone, which she'd switched off, had showed the temperature already at seventy as we arrived.

Then five minutes later the red Mustang pulled into the main parking lot from 235th northwest of where we huddled. Not exactly the kind of vehicle to fade into the background even out here. She buzzed down the windows on either side of the two-door, so it wouldn't get too hot while she waited, drumming fingers on the driver's door.

It wasn't long before a long-bed extended cab Ford 250 crept into the lot and stopped beside her with the rattle of its diesel engine dying down. The man who stepped from the driver's side was indeed Kane Kaslowski clad in khaki safari shirt and shorts who slapped on an Aussie hat he snugged up under his chin with a drawstring. His wife Ava dropped out the other side sporting a similar outfit complete, though, with a pith helmet featuring multiple vent holes, her short shorts with cuffs turned up further than his, showing off her tanned, well-toned legs. These clothes would have been fitting at an excavation site, I suppose, but seemed incongruous out here on a sports field whatever they were about to do.

Randi and I took this all in with a sense of uncertain anticipation. She crooked her head at me, lips pinched to one side as I peered through the small binoculars I'd drawn from my jacket pocket. She elbowed me, wanting her turn at the glasses. She strained on the lanyard still around my neck harder than necessary as it lashed across my Adam's apple. Did she suspect I'd lingered too long on Ava? She licked her lips. "He's handing over a bundle of cash," she whispered.

Without the aid of the glasses, I could see Mena stuff the wad into the bra beneath the long shirt hanging out over her pants, then offer the velvet pouch. Ava peeled the rim of the bag away to expose the diamond. It shone brightly, eerily shimmering into their faces from below casting them in unflattering shadows like something out of a black-and-white German expressionist film. Keeping it cupped in both hands for her husband, who gave it a cursory glance, she then slipped it back in the bag, opening the rear door to give to one of the two figures we could make out there now. The couple then went around to the truck bed and slid out a folding table, toting it to the ballfield at the easternmost edge of the park, unfolding the legs to set it down over the home plate of the baseball diamond freshly outlined in white. That location had the most unobstructed view of the rising sun, the starkly highlighted green grandstand a backdrop rising to the west.

"Now we should move closer," Randi whispered. We skulked past the booth to the storage shed and saw that we could use a couple of other outbuildings to hide behind as we advanced.

Meanwhile, the Kaslowskis marshalled their "troops," the two top students we could see were Sam Dekker and Elaine Schatz who lugged the electronic equipment to the rectangular table and emptied the gem now into a tray atop one of the machines.

In a broad-brimmed straw hat, Mena followed them, her blue denim shirt flapping its scooped hem over khaki-colored pants that billowed out from her thighs like jodh-purs, for God's sakes, as if she were going fox hunting. These people certainly weren't exactly veterans at clandes-tine skullduggery.

The two grad students in stonewashed jeans and baggy sweatshirts, academic uniforms of the day, I guess, dragged an extension cord to what looked like a seismometer or an oscilloscope by the squiggling line appearing on a hatch-marked round green screen and what must have been some kind of ore sampler, the tray where the diamond sat on a telescoping derrick-like pole, a green screen with a digital readout slanting out from its base. Sam, his angular face grizzled the way young women apparently preferred hand-some men these days, cranked the pole with the tray up about a meter or so.

The diamond in its perch caught the sun full on, something we could see better than they could since they were positioned underneath. “It looks like they’re preparing to measure any changes the jewel undergoes—if any,” I surmised.

Sine waves began to serpentine across the monitor beside the apparent ore sampler while Elaine, hair tied back in a ponytail, opened a laptop and began tapping in commands as Sam ran a camera recording this makeshift lab.

I checked my watch. “Ten after nine—twenty-eight minutes till solstice.”

Kane was gesturing upward at the height explaining something to the students though Mena was listening, too, staring up but seeing only wheel-like spokes of golden light streaming everywhere like a wild beacon as it caught and scattered the growing sunlight.

Maybe it was the flickering dazzle casting new shadows from the rising sun that made me catch something bobbing inside the Mustang.

“There!” I whispered, nodding towards the car. Its windshield glared back a bright reflection, making it difficult to see anything but a nebulous blob spring up inside.

She squinted. “Did she bring along a dog?”

Then we also noticed something emerge from the starker shadows behind the grandstand as if the darkness bulged out stringy fingers of tarry quagmire.

Tense, cocked like gun hammers ourselves behind the last shed, we watched two short masked figures in black jackets creep around the side of the grandstand's base, crouching towards where the archeologists had set up camp. I lifted the binoculars again. They were clearly armed with long-barreled pistols. Lugers? The jackets sported the same tiny logo on the breasts, the image of a broken Earth severed by a lightning bolt. GEOS! Then it hit home. "We weren't the only ones listening in last night," I muttered. Frantically, I lent Randi the binoculars again.

"Isn't that a little—well—gutsy?" she hissed.

"They're making a point," I said, "that they have a rightful claim?"

The archeologists, though, stayed focused on the screens, Elaine adjusting knobs to measure the diamond's reaction to the sun's rising intensity while Sam continued with the camcorder. They showed no signs of hearing the figures stalking them but the machines were making their own beeping, whirring noises now, too.

Then the shadow in the Mustang coalesced into something more substantial, a figure we finally recognized.

Randi blurted it out first as a question. "Matthew?"

"She picked up her husband!" I breathed out. Then I remembered a long-lost detail I should have realized before. Certain vintage models of the Shelby featured sequential taillights! "He had to be the one who left the note last night!"

"Nicky," she said, hunkering into an even tighter ball. "He's got a gun, too!"

"Those kids from GEOS can't know what the scientists are waiting for," I said.

"They'll ruin *everything*."

I gritted my teeth. "We have to halt this before they do."

Randi voiced the obvious. "How do you stop a runaway train?"

Our vantage point made it seem like we were watching a stage play. "What can we do?"

One of the two figures hobbled forward with a marked limp. A leftover from Thursday night's thwarted assault on the Huntingtons? That could give us a slight advantage. We'd take whatever we could get.

Side by side now, sharing a sideways glance at each other, the two stole past the grandstand taking advantage of the sharp metallic glare from the bleachers. The archeologists remained engrossed in whatever they hoped the sun might do to the diamond, granting a legend more credibility than it warranted, a weakness that clearly came with their profession.

"Uh, Nicky?" said Randi from our new vantage point. "We have another distraction besides the sun's magic we can call on."

"What?" I said distractedly, trying to see an opportunity that just wasn't there.

"My ace up the sleeve." She pointed downward, wavering her skirt so the seam partially parted.

"That's not up a sleeve!" I gaped. "You'd be putting yourself directly in the line of fire!"

"We can't wait for something that might never happen at zero hour," she said. "And that's assuming Lordy Vandemere over there won't prove a loose cannon."

"He already has. We can only hope he's mostly bluster."

Randi bored into my dubious assumption. "With a gun? And the poor archeologists aren't even armed!"

"Neither's Mena," I muttered. "I can at least cover you."

"You'd better," she smirked, "because I'm about to expose myself in the worst way."

"Or," I said with a half shake of my head, wishing we had a better alternative, "the best."

She looked at me with a tic at the edge of her lips that told me she liked the remark—and hated it at the same time. I withdrew the Glock from my holster with a soft slick of leather.

Matthew had already climbed out the passenger side of the Mustang, clicking the door shut using the flat of his hand to muffle it before wielding the gun with his other. Then he half-stooped along its side, between the truck, towards the Mustang's hood. The pistol's barrel glinted just for a second. It looked uncannily—and ironically—like an old-fashioned six-gun Colt Python Peacekeeper. A classic, to be sure, but it made him seem a dilettante more likely to have raided a museum than a gun shop.

"On the count of three?" I suggested as we both ducked down, ready to spring into action. "One—"

But just then the self-proclaimed assault couple from GEOS beat us to the punch. With the young man on point, the couple bolted out from the end of the fenced bull pen that led to the open field. They extended arms stiffly ahead, gripping the Lugers in their gloved hands, muzzles thinly black as they advanced into the sun's glare. The man, rail-thin himself, lips a blood-red slit in the ski mask, shouted, "Don't move or we'll *fire!*"

"Time to punt, Nicky!" said Randi and shot out from our corner of the shed like a tripped claymore.

"Not yet!" I cried through gritted teeth, clawing at air, but too late.

Briefly the Mustang and Ford blocked the intruders' view of us, too. Hard on her tail, I darted after her across the stretch of blacktop towards the grassy turf.

"The guy's mine," I said.

"No, no," she grimaced. "I've got more to bring to bear!"

I eyed her askance. He was maimed and maybe an easier target. But I knew what she meant. I couldn't match her arsenal by a long shot. She crossed right in front of me, while I cut left, confusing the two assailants with zigzagging targets, deflecting their attention from the archeologists and our client.

Then Randi, throwing herself full-force into the game again, slammed an arm down and whipped open her skirt, baring that gartered holster and in her vigor maybe too much more—her black bikini panties dazzling just as much as her glistening thighs, at the very moment the diamond from its lofty post began doing *something*. With a hiss from her lips, she zipped her pistol out, gripping it with both hands squarely aiming her weapon at her transfixed target, as he closed in on the far end of the table, mouth agape—as all of us were—but him stone still, helpless as Medusa's victim—although Randi cut a much more riveting figure. A strange tableau, Randi in a stand-off opposite the attacker in a far darker crouch, her skirt clinging open hung up on the lace of her panties, legs astride in her shiny boots as she tried not to waver in her stance.

Then she strained a look upward at the diamond beyond her reach, beyond everyone's.

That gave the young man's lady partner a chance to break from the frozen moment and twist towards Randi, as he did more slowly then, like mechanical figurines in a Glockenspiel.

Randi backed up only slightly, seeing that she hadn't held them off just yet but afraid to fire. I had to catch her back and somehow neutralize the girl even as Randi refused to retreat.

Then when the moment of solstice must have struck, the whole world exploded above us—but in a kaleidoscopic way that made everything play out in slow motion like we were all thrown underwater. For a second, the flash blinded everyone. But the bright light blasted Randi and me both backward. I caught myself, though, dropping to my knees, hands breaking my fall.

Randi wasn't so lucky. I saw her peripherally, dazzled by the ball of fire that spiraled in on itself rather than outward, more like a nucleus fusing. Crackling lightning lanced out everywhere from the top of that pole, where the diamond lay bursting out this more spectacular array. White smoke erupted upward amid golden beams, making a startling gem out of the sky itself, ending with a hypnotic flicker of plasma -like sprites, angelic threads that sprayed over us like gilded tinsel literally electrifying us, making everyone's hair flare. Then a single pin-thin red beam shot out the top of the short tower, the diamond's natural flaw intensified into a spindle skewering the blue zenith of the heavens. In its wake, a sizzling black tornado spewed out in a burgeoning cloud, producing a wind that battered us in the now-humid air, knocking Randi backwards so powerfully and swiftly, I couldn't catch her, unable to do anything but hunch further down to minimize the force of the blow.

The golden diamond, assuming a new life of its own, pulsed down fiery rays that scorched a series of images like black claws across the ground with a sizzling hiss. Then the jewel itself pitched from its cradle, arching down to strike the earth near us like a volcano's pyroclastic shrapnel, cratering blackness where it landed, steaming like fulgurite. The diamond sputtered forth crystal fire, a miniature swirling sun that at last spun to a tilting stop like a toy top.

What had just *happened*?

The thunderous explosion seemed to have rendered everything acoustically sharper, not deafening our hearing as we might have expected but honing it.

Kane leaped into action then, too, semaphoring his arms back and forth, yelling back, "We're not armed! And *look!*" He pointed down at the message emblazoned on the dirt beyond the grass. "*Pictographs*!!" Tentatively he edged from the table, bending to close in on the odd missive and maybe retrieve the diamond.

"Sam!" shouted the girl we thought was Elaine, trying to jerk her fellow student back away from the monitor they were manning.

"I have to cover this, Ell!" he said, shrugging her off frenetically, the camera burring as he persisted in swinging it slowly to and fro to record as much as he could.

"They've got real *guns*, Sam!" She grappled at the sharp collar of the shirt that stuck out the back of his sweatshirt, trying to yank him downward now.

Suddenly Kane recoiled, crying out in pain, dropping the diamond as quickly as he clambered to grasp it, palm raised displaying a fiery burn, rolling it even closer to Randi who lay flat on her back too far from me to reach.

From our perspective, we couldn't tell a thing about the ragged lines of the cypher, if that's really what it was. The diamond itself pulsated meretriciously like a crystal heart nearer the two of us than anyone else.

Kane, impelled by pain from the searing jewel and his own anger at these interlopers, took advantage of the stunned reaction to the pyrotechnics, regained his bearing just as the assailants were shaking their heads, blinking quickly and waving their guns, uncertain where the diamond had gone and where to refocus their attention. He jumped at the young man in the ski mask with the gimpy leg and body-tackled him, crying out with the pain in his hand, but with his other tearing at his balaclava, which the attacker struggled to keep on, but failing under Kane's surprising ferocity. Ava joined in to help her husband, grappling after the gun the assailant tried to fire but wildly now.

The graduate students took the cue from their bold mentor and leaped into action, too, grabbing at the female assailant who clicked the trigger, even as Sam shouldered her backward, the barrel flipped upward firing only at the sky. Elaine scrabbled to claw her balaclava off, too, sending the girl's long black hair flinging like snakes about her slender form, scratching the Oriental girl's face along her cheek that made her screech and glower madly even as they tousled her to the grass.

We'd fallen onto the open ground beyond the baseball diamond with nothing to block us, the wired backstop behind me. In the fray, we couldn't fire either for fear of injuring the innocents who had come to our aid before we could theirs. Mena still stood frozen on the far side of the table, torn between helping and recapturing the diamond that had already blistered Kane's hand. Matthew had scurried to her side, not knowing where the diamond was either but weaving the smoking barrel of his revolver limply at the tackled assailants. Thankfully, whatever he'd fired at he'd missed, puffs of smoke rising up in a couple of places nearby—and nowhere near anybody.

Randi lay splayed out like a runner who'd slid too far past home plate but backwards, skirt still stuck apart like a blown hatch that wouldn't close. She shifted the gun to her left hand, crabbing her right after the diamond, spidering fingers over the gem still sizzling in the dirt, then swiftly slipping it into her pocket with a harsh gasp. "Hole in one!" she croaked out though I could see she had singed the tips of her fingers.

"Wrong game!" I coughed back.

"Home run then?"

"Better," I burbled back, shaking my head at this insane exchange. We were too vulnerable out there in the open from the fusillade of bullets streaming from the attackers who kept clenching at the triggers despite efforts to pry their fingers loose. I had to take advantage of the archeologists wrestling with the assailants to cover Randi.

I juddered forward from my crouch like Frankenstein's monster before arching dolphin-like onto her with an unceremonious, "Ooooffff!" When I somehow caught my breath again, I gurgled out, "I covered you!"

"Oh, Nicky! You *covered* me!" I think we both meant different things. She was crying now, shedding real tears and trembling as she clamped me to her with both arms, the gun slinging from her limp wrist, the barrel banging at my arm.

And then she kissed me full on the lips!

In the distance the muted shattering of glass—and the useless clicking of triggers drawing on emptied magazines.

"My *car!*" Matthew bleated.

We both looked around, dazed. Stray bullets had cobwebbed the safety glass of the Mustang's windshield and punctured myriad holes in the side of the truck which blocked it.

That at least distracted Matthew from firing his gun again though he whipped that thing as though trying to throttle a serpent. But then, thankfully, he'd had only six bullets to the attackers' magazines which must have held at least ten rounds apiece. An arm about his wife's shoulder as they both slumped below the table, Mena was still looking in vain for the diamond, warily eyeing the downed bodies wrestling to disarm the assailants. Matthew, though, kept his eyes fixed on the car as though hoping it still offered a means of escape.

Elaine and Sam were both struggling to keep the thin girl in her would-be Ninja outfit pinned to the ground with their arms, Sam's especially long and lanky. But the lithe young woman would have none of it. In one desperate effort, she threw them both off her, like so much flotsam, acting the very Ninja she was costumed to be and scuttled over on all fours to aid her companion.

Sam then attempted to join his recovering mentor, Ava backing off as the two men tried to wrangle the Luger from the young man, the barrel still smoking and by now surely too hot to touch. The female assailant, though, whipsawed around and walloped both the men on top of her partner with whirling legs, sending them sprawling off before slamming the butt of her own Luger flat against the side of Sam's head, downing him instantly as his hand slapped at his bloodied temple. Then she was dragging her compatriot away from everyone.

I pushed up off Randi, checking to make sure I hadn't hurt her by landing so hard and that she hadn't been struck by any of the stray bullets. I reached down to pull her back up, knowing we somehow had to get back into the act. "You okay?"

Though she still looked stunned, she gave a jerky nod, struggling to close up her caught skirt but with a telling wince. "Just—very embarrassed." With a wry turn of her lips, she still managed to stress the last syllable. And she'd rebuked me for ill-timed humor! Still, it helped allay the awkwardness of all that had gone down in those last frenzied moments.

"The diamond?" I bowed down to make sure it wasn't catching her skirt on fire and hurting her further.

"Cooling a little, thank goodness," she breathed.

Then I twisted around towards the others where the melee had mercifully stopped, but with no clear winners. Kane and Sam both looked slack-jawed, eyes glazed over—but, even worse, defeated.

Kane, then shaking his head to recover, wrapped an arm around Sam, head bent, hand still trying to staunch the bleeding, favored his right hand by letting it hang before waving it at the ground. "We struck gold," he panted.

"Beyond our wildest dreams," Ava concurred nearby, as she and Elaine leaned against the table to steady themselves, too, before Ava pushed herself to stumble towards the apparent message in the dirt.

The assailants, still backing up, paused, spreading their legs wide and brandishing their empty guns again, trying to click in new magazines but failing even as they wheeled their arms towards Randi and me now. We raised the guns we hadn't even fired yet.

But then the absurdity of this showdown struck me. I had to shout it out loud. "Really?" I glared. "You want to end this with a shoot-out at the not-so-O.K. Corral?" I pointed to their jackets sporting the GEOS logos. "You're *scientists*, for God's sakes, about to gun down fellow scientists?!"

Then the voice of sanity whispered in my ear like my own personal Jiminy Cricket, though far prettier. "Really, Nicky? You're going to *talk* them to death to win this little kerfuffle?"

I couldn't help smirking at her choice of words, because it did seem like that despite the lethal weapons bandied about so blithely. The archeologists and their students also gawked at me as dumbfounded as Mena and her husband.

The two assailants unmasked now, the girl dabbing at the scratch across her face, flared their nostrils. "You haven't heard the last of this!" the girl said through bared teeth.

"There's more at stake than you know," her companion

affirmed thinly, lowering the barrel of his Luger—but resolutely slapping in another magazine at last. The girl followed suit. But they stopped aiming the weapons at us, reason somehow prevailing since they hadn't secured the booty they'd come for and didn't realize that Randi had.

Diplomat par excellence? *Me?!* Even if this were a temporary victory, we'd at least avoided a pointless bloodbath. Well, except for Sam's wound.

The assailants retreated to the grandstand and hoisted heavy machines out of the darkness where they'd been waiting all along, firing up engines that thundered with a throaty roar we felt underfoot. The motorcycles looked much bulkier than Harley-Davidsons, tailpipes shining like tin cannons, obviously much-modified. The same rumbling I'd heard outside Randi's apartment last night?

The young man shook a fisted arm in the air. Then making wheelies as if they were horses rearing up on hind legs, they raced off defiantly in clouds of billowing smoke trailing a glittering burst of brilliant flaming blasts from exhausts that propelled them forward more like rockets, firing Parthian shots fiercely up at the bright sky rather than back at us.

As we both gawked side by side at this ferocious, if futile, show of force, Randi surprised everyone more by abruptly crumpling at my feet like a rag doll!

23

"I'm *not* the kind of girl who *faints!*" Randi insisted, when she woke later after I'd carried her to the van and laid her gently into the passenger seat.

I looked her over again for a wound I might have missed, still astonished no one had been shot. "You sure?"

Ava peered into the still-open door behind me. "You had us worried back there, honey."

Kane added, "We thought for sure you'd caught a bullet! That kid wouldn't stop firing."

"You were so brave," Elaine lauded Randi. "I mean, flashing everybody and standing there like Catwoman with her claws out?!"

More than just claws, I thought. But I couldn't help but gloat. "She loves a dramatic entrance."

"Oh, you!" Randi tried to ball up a small fist and slug me again, but flinched at the effort, pulling back. "My God! I ache all over!" She scowled at me wryly. "You jumped me like the Incredible Hulk!"

The other girls laughed outside the van, Mena venturing a brittle smile though she hadn't said much at this point, looking guilty, but maybe just a little contrite.

"I didn't 'jump' jump you,' sweetie," I said in my best Phil Donahue voice. "I was shielding you."

"But with the force of a fullback," she groaned. "And my God, does my heinie hurt!" Of course that was due as much to the storm the diamond had unleashed. She started to feel her backside but realized it would be awkward to do so in front of everybody, even more so, I suspected, because touching there wouldn't make it any better.

Mena glanced at her watch, then at Matthew. "We might still make the ceremony. I have to be there by noon no matter what."

Matthew said, "How are we going to explain the car damage?"

"An accident?" she tried. "That's no lie."

Kane looked around. "I think the rest of us have a pretty good reason why we won't show." He nodded at Randi and me. "You two above all."

"Just tell them we've got the diamond and will return it soon," I said to Mena.

She nodded, wringing her hands. "You aren't going to—"

I shook my head. "Client-agent privilege," I said, oversimplifying the circumstances.

Mena looked dispirited, not responding yet.

I raised my eyebrows. "Along with their daughter back in

the fold?"

She finally managed, "You must think me just another poor spoiled rich brat."

Randi looked at me self-consciously a second before shifting her eyes towards Mena. "Don't you think it's about time you opened up more with your folks about how you feel, you know, to clear the air? It might bring you closer. A little counseling wouldn't hurt all of you either."

I looked at Randi, surprised and proud. Miranda Degrotti, psychologist now? "You're giving Charlie Brown's Lucy a run for her five cents!"

Mena tried another half-smile that twitched. "The condition," she said softly, "for your silence?"

"It's up to you," I said. "You might even try some diplomacy with GEOS since you must have promised the people behind Project Thunderstone something like you did these folks."

Mena protested, "After what they did here?"

"They must have acted under orders," said Randi. "It looked like you just forgot them."

"This chance came up pretty fast," said Mena. "There wasn't time to explain. And they couldn't insure the diamond's safety anyway."

"I'm not sure we did any better," Kane offered, "though the diamond seemed better than ever now."

Randi patted at her pocket. "Whatever happened, it's still the hardest known substance on earth."

But I was looking at Mena now, too. "You could just give the people at GEOS back their money. That would wipe the slate clean—and make them look elsewhere." I pointed at the road where we'd seen the motorcycles all but take off into the air. "They seem to be doing just fine with whatever mysterious resources they've already scrounged up."

Mena looked agog at the suggestion, Matthew merely angry.

"You don't have to worry about us, dear," said Kane to Mena. "We've gotten more than our ten-grand worth."

"And enough work ahead," agreed his wife with a nod back out to the curious cryptograph, "for maybe the next five years. Plus I'll bet there'll be a monograph or two in our future somewhere."

"Not to mention," Sam proposed, "another major dig if you're really lucky?"

Kane gazed out towards the sun rising higher into a sky such a cobalt blue that it seemed more like a painting. "We can't underestimate our ancestor's potential for tapping into natural, or should I say supernatural, resources we're only beginning to fathom ourselves."

Randi chimed in. "But look at what all of you did on your own today, pitching in like this. You saved our—" She caught herself from actually saying the word outright. "Well, maybe not *my* particular 'asset,' but everybody else's here."

"Don't underestimate your part in saving the day, too," Kane added.

"It was quite a show of power, wasn't it," I joked about Randi's role.

"More than I planned on, that's for sure," Randi said, reddening.

We all laughed awkwardly, a welcome relief, though, from the morning's tension.

"I guess these clothes are headed for the wash again—along with me." Randi started to shake her head but stopped suddenly, lolling to the side.

"Whoa there, girl," I said reaching to stop her from toppling. "You're still wobbly."

"Maybe a little," she said, struggling to recover. "But I'm tougher than I look."

We all laughed at her latter-day protestation. "In the end?" I quipped.

"Nicky!" she chastened, love-tapping my arm more solidly this time. A good sign?

"A shower and some rest," I said, "and you should be ready to take on the world again."

"It did feel a little like that's what we were doing here," she said. "But you're forgetting something else that'll help." She touched her lips.

"You're hungry after all this?" Kane smirked with a conspiratorial look at his wife. That covered a lot of bases. I think he meant it to.

"I should say so," Randi demurred with that little-girl look again meaning something else only I understood.

I tried to smooth over the gray area there. It was getting to be my prime directive as a detective. Everybody had been too busy during the melee to see her kiss me, and my being overwhelmed by her clenching me to her. "She has an appetite that won't quit." I left it at that.

"In a way we all do, don't we," said Ava, holding her husband's hand but glancing back at the message on the ground.

I stared longer myself at the strange burn marks the diamond's fired brightness had left there. "Any idea from past experiences what that might mean?"

"Hard to tell whether that's just an accident of nature," said Kane, "or an intentional code of some kind."

Ava tilted her head at her husband. "Diamonds often feature inclusions that could have caused this to look like a message," mused Ava. "You know, like seeing a 'face' on the surface of Mars that turns out to be a natural rock formation? We won't know until we study it further. But damn. Doesn't the pattern there look like cuneiforms??"

"With all those twists and turns," Kane mused angling his head at the blackened earth, "it could even be a map to a labyrinth or tunnel somewhere."

Sam elevated the camera. "We've got a record to study to our heart's content in the months to come."

"Is it possible," Randi speculated herself now, "it could show the way to the missing statue of the goddess Lakshmi—or maybe even her other 'eye'?"

"Maybe, girl," beamed back Kane, "you're in the wrong field! Kolimar *was* the name of a famous Indian diamond mine tapped out and lost over time."

I felt obliged to add a little reason to the conjectures. "But embedding a real 'missive' inside the hardest known natural substance known to man? That's impossible, isn't it??"

Ava shrugged but Ellen looked at Sam and spoke up herself. "We may be just starting out in this business, but we've already seen astounding things when it comes to the magic cultures believed their artifacts could capture."

A long space of silence while all of us entertained our own thoughts and, in my case, considerable doubts. "Regardless," I finally said, "you'll keep us apprised of your progress?"

"Whether you like it or not," Kane grinned, "you're part of this motley family of ours now."

"More than you realize," said Mena. "You'll get your bonus—and then some. My father can be quite generous when he wants to be. And getting back that diamond?" She shook her head with that tired, close-mouthed smile. "He's promised at least to get you invited to a special showing at the Pearl Gallery through the Fourth of July that'll include one of his paintings."

Randi and I glanced at each other skeptically. "As guests," she said, "or watchdogs?"

Mena pinched her thin lips together. "You know Daddy. He likes killing two birds with one stone."

I groaned. "Can't you think up a less violent cliché?"

"Sorry, but that's one of his favorite sayings. Opening night at least should be an elegant soiree next weekend, though Matt and I can't make it."

"Oh, Nicky," said Randi. "Another excuse to get all dressed up?"

"As if you needed one," I laughed. "Meanwhile, you

have to recuperate from this little showstopper of yours." I frowned down at the scorched earth. "One thing's for certain. We can't leave tracks like this behind."

"I've got some tools in the truck," Kane assured me. "Since we have a digital record of it now, we can rake away the worst." The smell in the air lingered but the explosive flash of the sunlight on the diamond had remarkably left little other evidence behind.

"The only other problem might be the shattered glass of the Mustang," I pointed out.

But Matt stared over at the car grimly. "The saving grace of safety glass."

"We've got some brushes that'll take away any remnants," said Ava mustering forces with Elaine and Mena.

"I doubt we'll find all the empty shells," Kane remarked picking up some with his good hand but getting Sam to help, too.

"Just do what we can," I said, "and hope nobody looks too closely." Despite what CSI programs depicted, that sometimes was the case even with established crime scenes.

When I thought we'd done our best, I thanked them all for their help and slipped around to the driver's seat of the van.

Randi patted the pocket of her skirt. "We've even saved Sari Maravar's bacon. She'll have reason to party, too."

I crooked my head at her as I turned the key to the ignition. "Her—*party*? Maybe in another of her lifetimes." We both laughed thinly as we watched everyone return to their vehicles. Matt looked surprised that the Mustang started up, despite the damage it had sustained, Mena trying to temper his disgruntled look. They had a lot to deal with later.

Once their team examined the bullet holes to make sure none had pierced the gas tank, Kane brought the Ford's noisy diesel engine back to life, too, everyone taking their place back inside with their equipment ready for the adventure of figuring out what they had gathered here.

Color was beginning to return to Randi's face as we waved at the rest, the first to leave since we were closest to the southern entrance.

Would we ever see them again despite the friendly amenities? That remained to be seen.

But then we, too, had our own personal issues to wrap up.

Epilogue

She settled herself carefully into the bucket seat, saying, "The cool leather feels good." Partial shade from nearby bushes had protected the van.

"Cold pack when we get you home then?" I said.

"I was thinking more like a hot bath."

"Cold might reduce the swelling if you have any."

"I'm sure it's a different kind of 'gold' down there. Mixed with more black and blue— Well, you're not going to be ogling my backside anytime soon."

"Think again!" I retorted. "Our skin's the only organ that always regenerates. You'll be back to your old self soon."

"Now you're an expert on matters of the flesh?"

"Only as a layman," I grinned.

"Oh, Nicky! You never quit, do you!"

"Neither do you."

She paused. "You said 'home.' Mine or yours?"

"You want me to take you back to your apartment?"

She idly picked at the dirt on her skirt though it didn't help much. "I guess I should."

"You can stay with me a while," I said. "I'll take you

back later?" I didn't want to push her.

"I need to get cleaned up, though, and so should you."

"You said something about having dessert today at your place."

"I'm not sure I'm up to that now. I wasn't planning on being this bunged up, though I guess it's better than being grazed by a bullet like before."

"You can get cleaned up at my place, then we'll 'decompress' together. We should celebrate somehow, don't you think, since we'll be getting our 'just deserts' from the Huntingtons at least."

Her voice was small when she answered, not meeting my eyes, "Okay."

After I pulled into the garage and felt that home was somehow different now that I was there with her, I helped ease her out to let her into the utility room where she noticed the machines. "You mind me washing these clothes here then? I don't want to get your furniture dirty."

"I'm a guy, sweetie. I'm not as punctilious as you are."

"'Punctilious,'" she mocked me lightly again. "You're so cute." She tickled a finger along the side of my cheek. It felt good.

"I can wash them for you while you get cleaned up in the main bath and I shower in mine."

"Won't that make you run out of hot water?"

"We put in a 75-gallon water heater," I said, "but the washer's on the 'warm/cold' setting anyway so don't worry. Just leave your clothes outside the door."

"You always seem anxious to get me out of my clothes."

I tilted my head. "Aren't I just doing what you asked?"

"Now who's being the little imp?"

But that made me blush. "I'll get a robe for when you come out. Will that make it better?"

"It's already too warm in here for a robe."

"I never turn on the air-conditioning until late in the afternoon. Will one of my shirts do instead?"

"If it's long enough, maybe with tails?"

"I'll come up with something."

"You have some Woolite?" she said.

"What do you need that for if I'm doing the wash?"

"I can scrub my underthings by hand in the bathroom sink. I got pretty sweaty up here." She indicated her breasts. "And remember, that blast sent me sliding backwards on my skirt, panties—the whole schmeer."

"'Smear' is right," I said, seeing that her reeling backwards from the blast had soiled her more than she thought.

"A warm/cold wash would be okay but they need to be in a lingerie bag, bra clasped and everything."

I showed her the mesh bag at the bottom of the laundry basket where Angie had left it.

"You do seem equipped with everything," she smirked. "But they'll still need to be air-dried. They're cotton and polyester."

"I'll hang them on a laundry rack over the heat register there," I said, pointing. "You've stashed spares in your purse anyway now, right?"

She hesitated. "I do—but these go better with this outfit."

"I got it," I smiled.

"Don't forget, Nicky, to take the diamond out of the skirt's pocket. We can't risk washing away its 'magic.'"

"As if that'll ever happen." Although I did sometimes forget to take things out of my own pockets, I wouldn't have forgotten *that*.

I picked up the clothes she left in a pile outside the door in the hall, knocked on the door to give her a white Arrow dress shirt I seldom wore anymore. She reached out a bare arm and took the hanger. As I prepared my load of wash and threw in her clothes, I noticed her panties had 'Sunday' scripted across them. In the melee, I'd somehow missed that. I shook my head at her charming predilections with a complacent smile, then applied Shout to the grass and dirt smudges and rubbed them away between my hands, removing the diamond from her skirt and pocketing it for now in my jacket. It still felt warm. From the experiment this long afterwards, or the radiation? Maybe both?

I heard her turn on the bathtub faucet rather than the shower head. She had the time for that now.

I mixed a load of my clothes in with hers, including what I was wearing, padding back out in my robe to start the machine before returning to the master bath for a shower. Afterwards, I felt renewed as I slipped on clean underwear and stepped into gray Wranglers with a blue turtleneck, leaving the stone in the jacket that I hung up for now.

I heard her still idly sloshing in the bathtub as I went into the living room to prepare the sofa for her with a blanket, some pillows and the cold rag before moving the clothes to the dryer except for her underwear which I hung over a register.

It was over an hour later before she tiptoed out from the bathroom barefoot, the shirt's sleeves dangling past her hands partly because the cuffs needed links to close them, the long, scooped tails front and back covering her more than adequately.

"There's room enough for two in here!"

"I weighed a little more before Angie died," I said tersely.

She made a sympathetic move of her mouth, then turned around, looking over her shoulder. "You can't see anything, right?"

"You're safe," I smirked.

"Really? Says the guy who looks like a cat licking his chops at a bowl of milk?"

"God, I can't be that obvious!"

"Almost," she said, lips puckered as she hesitated at the couch.

"Would you rather rest up in the spare bedroom?"

"I'd rather be out here with you. I won't stay too long, just until my underwear dries."

"This sounds vaguely familiar," I said.

"Doesn't it though."

"I'd like it if you stayed longer." I said it as a question, though.

"You're not getting tired of me?"

"Unless you're getting tired of me."

"That's not going to happen anytime soon." She paused. "As long as you don't call the office and check the answering machine for messages. Enough with the working dinner routine for a while. After all, it *is* Sunday."

"Your panties made sure I knew that," I grinned.

"You didn't notice when I was out there exposed in front of God and everybody?"

"We were kind of preoccupied with saving a lot of things in case you hadn't noticed." But I looked at her. "So never on Sunday? Sounds like a plan."

"It's settled then." She plopped a pillow down over her lap, staring at the cold pack warily. "That hot bath soaked away a lot of the soreness."

"Cold might accelerate the healing more."

"I don't know, Nicky," she said not hiding the whine in her voice very well.

I pointed to the gel pack. "Just give it a try. I can get you some cocoa to keep you warm. I have an instant hot water tap."

She hesitated. "You have any malted milk?"

"Is instant Ovaltine okay? Malted milk's in it."

"Sounds perfect." She picked up the ice pack uncertainly and opened up the comforter to cover herself.

I smiled. "Coming right up, m'lady." She smiled at my gentlemanly greeting and genteel bow. But truth be told, she acted more a "lady" than "Lady Mena" ever had—even sans panties.

When I returned with the mug which she took in both hands, she shivered with a "Brrr!", adding, "Get your cute butt over here and help keep me warmer."

"Yes, ma'am." I sat next to her as she squirmed.

"I can't take much more of this, Nicky."

"I thought you said you had a high tolerance for pain."

"Not when I can stop it anytime on my own!" She scooted forward with a wince while struggling to yank the cold pack up from her backside with one hand and balancing the mug with the other. That caused her to ruffle up the tail of the shirt which I hastily tried to flip back down while I took the gel away. But not before I caught a look at the number she'd done on her bottom, a yellow-black splotch down from the tail of her spine. And then I glimpsed something else and couldn't stop myself from blurting out delightedly, "*Dimples?!*"

"Nicky!" she giggle-squealed, sweeping a hand back there with a grimace to make sure I couldn't see any more.

"I'm just detecting," I joked.

"You promised we'd have the rest of the day off!"

I came back with the remark she'd used earlier for me. "But they're so *cute!*"

The blush suffused her whole face, making her even prettier. "You've seen too much of me lately—and in the worst way."

"A matter of opinion."

She cast a more coquettish glance at me. "I *like* dressing for you, not *un*dressing. So why am I doing so much of that lately?"

"Just lucky?"

She jabbed at me. "You really *are* a smooth operator!"

As she leaned into me, I raised my hand over the back of the sofa so she could rest more easily, accidentally brushing her neck. "My gosh, Nicky, your hands are so cold!"

"The gel," I apologized, recalling my mother's favorite bromide to add, "but doesn't that mean a warm heart?"

She gave an exasperated click of her lips. "What's a girl to do with you anyway?"

I Groucho-Marxed my eyebrows.

"Don't *do* that, Nicky!" she giggled again but more easily now, the flat of her free hand over her abdomen. "I wouldn't want to turn your lovely blue couch *green!*" Only someone so obsessed with color coordination would have put it like that!

"But I've got an idea how we can celebrate today."

She lowered her eyes at me. "I'll bet you do!"

"I didn't mean *that*," I spluttered. "I was thinking after you get some rest, maybe I could barbecue us some salmon and asparagus out on the patio with a little merlot?"

"You're tempting me again."

"That's the whole idea," I smiled.

"Go see how my underwear's doing so I can get out of this shirt and into some decent clothes then. And come back soon to keep me warm—and I'll return the favor for your hands."

"Deal!"

She tittered, a hand curled girlishly at her lips once more.

It was too warm for the furnace to click on, though, so her underthings were still too damp. Instead, I brought her back something else that I wanted her to see for herself.

"You'll have to go without a little longer," I said, "or settle for underwear that doesn't match."

She recoiled. "Why are you carrying *that* out here?"

"An expensive hand warmer?" I opened my palm. "I wanted your opinion."

"It looks *different* somehow."

"That's what I thought." But then I placed it in her palm. "But do you feel that?"

She looked up at me. "Could it be?"

"I know," I said. "It's *vibrating.*"

She shuddered differently now. "Take it *away,* Nicky—and let's get back to where we were."

I plucked it up and hid it back in my jacket in the bedroom before resuming my place beside her. She sidled closer, bringing her legs up under the comforter and smoothing it over her hips, taking the weight off her bottom so it was against the back of the couch instead. "Mmm."

"Better?"

"Uh-huh." Sleepily she added, "I should practice what I preached to Mena about opening up more."

"You've opened up plenty lately, little lady," I quipped with apologies to John Wayne.

"Not that way, silly. I mean, I don't want to keep things secret from you anymore."

I brushed golden strands away from her eyes and lips where they were sticking from her getting them damp in the bath. "You don't have to tell me anything you don't want to."

"That's all the more reason why I've got to say what you might not like."

"I like everything about you so far, sweetie." I'd already

said more than I should have.

"Remember I mentioned earlier that—there's 'another'?"

My smile faltered, heart at my throat. "You've got a boyfriend after all?"

She shook her head. "You're the only guy in my life now. But there *is* 'another.'"

"'Another' what?" I said, a hand clenched on the sofa's arm.

She nuzzled closer, smacking her lips together, the loose cuff of the shirt flopping as her injured fingers crossed my chest, then muttered it so softly I almost didn't hear her. "Another *me*!"

And before I could ask her what she meant, she was breathing quietly like a baby again, her sweet warm breath at my heart.

Bewildered as I was, I felt strangely content now that I had her cradled again in my arm, thinking that things hadn't just come to a close, but might be only beginning.

Nick Christmas

Returns in…

Recovering the Nude

Steel heiress Madeline Pfizer's grandchildren hire Nick Christmas and his Girl Friday Randi to recover the $10 million original Gérôme painting of the nude Galatea purchased at the Pearl Gallery exhibition they attended in Portland, Oregon. A sabotage attempt on the detective agency can't stop them pursuing such suspects as curator Gayle Manyon, her protege and the heiress' caregiver. Meanwhile, the gallery hosts a Marilyn Monroe look-alike contest to highlight a mysterious new exhibit scheduled for the July 4th gala when the winner's chosen. During the festivities, the real nature of the theft is revealed just as stalkers nab the new exhibit and the winner while Nick and company fight to stop them.

About the Author

AUTHOR PHOTOGRAPH BY RICK PAULSON

A former Fulbright, NDEA Fellow, college teacher and professional film reviewer, Steve Dimeo has over the last 40 years published articles, reviews, fiction and poetry in various literary and national journals. An award winning novelist, he has written 28 novels, with his Nick Christmas mysteries featuring science fiction or supernatural touches and the witty repartee in a budding May-December romance between the detective and his "girl Friday." Search for the Golden Diamond of Kolimar is the second novel in the Nick Christmas Mysteries series.

Steve enjoys hour-long morning walks besides writing (which he's done since age twelve), reading suspense novels, watching classic films, cooking simple, healthy meals, and remember good times with his late wife Nettie for over 27 years.

CPSIA information can be obtained
at www.ICGtesting.com
Printed in the USA
BVHW08s0533100718
520936BV00001B/5/P

9 781609 752217